TOP TEN TIPS FOR FAIRY GODMOTHERS IN THE MORTAL WORLD

10. Get plenty of sleep—you'll need it for the long, lonely nights ahead of you.

9. Don't watch any movies starring Mel Gibson, Sean Connery or Tom Cruise.

8. Cancel your subscription to the Sinfully Sweet lingerie catalog.

7. Let down your hair *only* when it's time for a shampoo.

6. Tell him you're allergic to flowers.

5. Tell him chocolate makes you break out.

4. Don't *ever* let him catch you staring into his sky-blue eyes.

3. When you swoon, be sure he's not there to catch you.

2. At all costs, avoid diaper-clad cherubs brandishing bows and arrows.

And if all else fails, remember the Number-One tip:

1. FAIRY GODMOTHERS MUST *NOT* FALL IN LOVE!

Dear Reader,

Love! It's inspired thousands of songs, movies and books. It's what we dream about, talk about and read about. But what makes it so special? Mary Anne Wilson answers that very question this month in this special Valentine's Day book, *Valentine for an Angel*.

Many of you may remember the heroine, Angelina, from Mary Anne's previous American Romance *Mismatched Mommy*. This time, it's Angelina's turn to find true love.

From Mary Anne Wilson and me—and all of us at Harlequin—HAPPY VALENTINE'S DAY!

Best,

Debra Matteucci
Senior Editor & Editorial Coordinator
Harlequin Books
300 East 42nd Street
New York, NY 10017

Valentine for an Angel

MARY ANNE WILSON

Harlequin Books

TORONTO • NEW YORK • LONDON
AMSTERDAM • PARIS • SYDNEY • HAMBURG
STOCKHOLM • ATHENS • TOKYO • MILAN
MADRID • WARSAW • BUDAPEST • AUCKLAND

ISBN 0-373-16714-8

VALENTINE FOR AN ANGEL

This edition published by arrangement with Harlequin Books S.A.

® and TM are trademarks of the publisher. Trademarks indicated with
® are registered in the United States Patent and Trademark Office, the
Canadian Trade Marks Office and in other countries.

Printed in U.S.A.

Prologue

February 12th, 4:00 a.m.,
Santa Barbara, California

As she came to him again, the deep void of sleep was gone, filled with the sense of her presence in his dreams. She was coming closer and closer, her presence so strongly surrounding him that he couldn't move. He couldn't wake up. He didn't want to wake up. He simply waited for her.

She drew closer and closer until her image materialized in front of him. Yet he couldn't really see her. He sensed her. He sensed softness, gentleness, a heat that seeped into his soul, a scent that tickled at his memory, yet never quite found a name.

He knew she was someone he needed. Someone he wanted. Someone who owned part of his soul. He couldn't make out her features, yet he knew she was all joy and desire, wisps of substance and passion, of need and fulfillment.

His body began to anticipate more than the swirling sensations she brought with her, more than this sense of her hovering just out of his reach. Tension grew in him, an ache surfaced, but when he reached out, there was nothing. She slipped back away from him, back to the fringes of his consciousness, fading into a place where he couldn't follow. The way she had done over and over again in the dreams he'd been having for the past month.

The next moment, he was instantly awake, abruptly facing the reality of being in his own bed, in his own house on the bluffs above the Pacific, and filled with an aching loss, a sense of frustration that defied explanation. Over it was a loneliness that blanketed him, suffocated him, overwhelmed him.

Dennis Benning took a deep, shaky breath and lay very still, feeling the havoc the dream had played with his body. He flexed his clenched hands open on the sheets by his side, and exhaled again, hoping to ease the tautness that was almost painful to him. If the dream woman had been there right then, if she'd been real, flesh and blood, lying with him in the softness of the night, he would have taken her in a heartbeat. He groaned softly as that idea only made his discomfort grow.

As he exhaled, he muttered, "Get a grip. It's just a dream, a damned dream." He eased his eyes open, hoping to stop the inevitable visions that came when he thought of the woman. But that simple action stopped nothing.

At the foot of the bed, in front of the French doors where pale moonlight filtered into the room, he saw her again. The merest suggestion of a substance, the illusion of the woman as if formed in wisps of dispersing smoke. A slender vision in a long, flowing gown, her hair cascading around her shoulders in a riot of curls, her face a blur. As he watched, the vision floated silently higher and higher, until it disappeared into the shadows of the ceiling.

There was only the whisper of a breeze in its wake, and for a single heartbeat he thought he caught the scent of flowers, no, the sweetness of a meadow on a summer's day. But as he blinked and took a shuddering breath, that was gone too. Gone as surely and as completely as the lingering remnants of a dream, trailing away when consciousness pushed it back to where it belonged.

He sank back into the bed, into linen damp from the heat that drenched his body. A dream, a dream that slipped from one craziness into another. But it was over.

There was nothing there now, nothing, just the night and the muffled sounds of the Pacific far below the place on the bluffs where his house had been built. There was no woman. Nothing. He was completely alone.

He exhaled slowly, and the only reality of the dream was the lingering of the physical effect it had on his body. He closed his eyes tightly, willed himself to relax, and knew the dream wouldn't reoccur tonight. It never happened twice in one night. Not even every night. Just unexpectedly, right when he'd thought it was gone for good. Then it came back softly and surely, until he was lost in it.

Crazy, he thought, to be longing for a dream to return. Just crazy. But as he began to tumble into the grayness of sleep returning, he had an even crazier thought. He knew the woman in his dreams. He knew her well. But he'd never met her.

Chapter One

February 12th, 7:00 p.m.

"Obsessive-compulsive," Angelina muttered to herself, not quite understanding that technical human term, but somehow knowing it fit her actions where Dennis Benning was concerned.

What she did understand was the fact that for the past month something had been drawing her back to the man, to check on him, just to reassure herself that he was doing well. She justified it by remembering how much he'd been through in the past six months. Two lost loves, the discovery of a half brother he had never known existed. So, she checked on him.

She'd look in on him while he slept in those quiet hours before dawn, then she would make herself leave, telling herself he was fine, that she didn't have to go back again. But she did go back, again and again. And this time, she hadn't waited for the slow hours.

It was only seven o'clock in the evening when she

found him in his offices on the tenth floor of an older building in the downtown section of the city.

"Brother, you look tired." His half brother, Sam, studied him intently. "What's going on with you?"

Angelina frowned at Dennis as she hovered just above him. Tired? Yes, he did look tired. She didn't know how she had missed that.

Sam leaned forward, pressing his hands flat on the thick law books that littered Dennis's desk and lifting one eyebrow in his brother's direction. The two men could have been mirror images, almost. Not quite.

Angelina had always felt Dennis was what she supposed a human woman would think of as very attractive. Sam, too, but even though the men reflected the same general looks, she saw such differences in them.

Sam was the rougher version of Dennis. The unfinished version, maybe. Dennis was the end product without flaws. Tall, blond, lean, with a touch of tan to his skin, pleasingly even features and the bluest eyes. Oh, he'd changed since her first contact with him. The sandy hair was longer, almost brushing the collar of his chambray shirt. Even the shirt was a change, from three-piece suits and buttoned-downs to casual cotton and jeans.

He'd gone from tax attorney for one of the best firms in Santa Barbara, to starting his own firm, where his primary client now was his brother. He took care of Sam's contracts in the movie industry, helped negotiate them, helped with investing and taxes. The two men, even though they'd only met two months ago, were closer than most humans. A good thing, she thought, especially when Dennis was about to start the most important phase of his life. Or, actually, had already started it.

It pleased Angelina that he'd been moving away from the mind-set of being a "Benning," from being part of a family whose heritage was in the upper crust of Santa Barbara society. He was a changed person, and she liked that change very much.

"I'm not getting much sleep," Dennis murmured, a wry half smile playing at the corners of his mouth and getting all of her attention. "I've been having these dreams."

Sam looked about as taken aback as Angelina felt. Dreams?

"Dreams?" Sam echoed.

Dennis shrugged, testing the fabric of the shirt he wore open at the throat and with the sleeves rolled back over his forearms. "Crazy, isn't it? I don't ever remember dreaming before, not really."

"What sort of dreams? Monster dreams or what Mikey calls his circus dreams, where the clowns are after him?"

Dennis sat back in his chair. "Oh, not clown dreams. These dreams are..." He sighed as he clasped his hands behind his head and gave his brother a slanted look. "I guess you'd call them sort of erotic."

Erotic dreams?

"Erotic dreams?"

Angelina had been there last night, but she hadn't sensed him dreaming and certainly not having erotic dreams. She should have known. She would have. Then she understood. Whomever Miss Victoria had assigned to the Francine Clark-Dennis Benning intersection, must already be at work. Dreams were a big factor in many human pairings, a way to get the other person into the thoughts of the soon-to-be lover.

She drew back as Dennis smiled, and was more than a bit thankful that Miss Victoria hadn't given her the assignment. She knew right then she'd become too involved with the Clarks and the people in their lives, the people like Dennis Benning.

"Not really. Just they could be erotic if they kept going," he said.

"And that's why you're worn out when they're over?"

Too involved by far. In that moment, she knew she wouldn't be back to check on Dennis. No more watching him sleep and having to slip away when she'd forget and begin to materialize in his room. No, she wouldn't be back here. She had no place here at all. Everything was under control.

The smile crinkled his eyes at the corners, and she knew her decision to leave was the right one. "These aren't peaceful dreams," Dennis said. "They're as frustrating as hell."

"So, who's the lady frustrating you? Oh, never mind. I know. It's obvious. Francine, isn't it?"

"You know more than I do. The woman's there, and I know her, but I don't know her." Dennis sighed, then sat back in his chair.

"Trust me, those Clark sisters can drive you crazy, and they're sexy as hell."

"Yeah, you're right," he said. "Now, why don't you tell me what you're doing in these parts, and without your new bride?"

"Melanie's with Reggie and the new baby at her mom's house. I'm picking her up there, then we're going to the restaurant. I was driving past and thought I'd see if you were still working, which you are, and if you wanted to ride over with me so you can pick up Francine."

"Oh, man, I forgot all about dinner," Dennis muttered as he took a quick look at his watch. "I'm snowed under here. You don't suppose—?"

"No, I don't suppose. You need a break, and it isn't all bad to spend time with the woman of your dreams."

Dennis stood to face his brother. "I knew I shouldn't have told you about them."

"It's good to know you dream," Sam said. "Now, let's get out of here."

Dennis flicked off the light at his desk, then went around to where Sam stood. "Who's coming to this dinner?"

"Ben, Reggie, Mel and me, you, Francine."

"Mother and Father aren't invited, are they?"

Sam shook his head at the mention of the Bennings. "No. I stopped by there this afternoon and your mother had retired to her room after suffering one of those spells she does so well. When she found out you were seeing Francine for dinner, she couldn't bear it." Sam tapped Dennis on the shoulder. "That woman is incredible. She leads our father on a merry chase, all the while muttering something about the Clarks having a dozen kids and everyone of them is invading her life like a plague of rabbits."

Angelina cringed when Dennis smiled a bit tightly. "Yes, Mother's unique, that's for sure."

"I believe our father said she thinks she's a pariah in this town, and that the Bennings are the laughing-stock of the social elite."

Dennis snapped open a briefcase sitting on one of the chairs by the desk and slipped a few papers into it. "One thing you'll learn being around us very long. Mother survives." He snapped the briefcase shut and turned to Sam. "She's tough as nails, de-spite her little spells that she can produce at will. The woman's got stamina, if nothing else."

The man was an incredible human being. He was saddled with a mother who was so dependent on her social position that any breath of what she perceived as scandal, became a major calamity for everyone in her vicinity. He had a father who indulged that mother. Yet Dennis was so normal for a human, such an endearing creature.

She didn't realize that she'd moved closer to him until she was startled by the hint of the aftershave he always wore. But that was impossible. She was ob-serving, not experiencing, yet it was there when she inhaled. The scent.

Then he ran his free hand over his hair, mussing it slightly, and she shocked herself by impulsively reaching out to smooth it. A foolish thing to do, since her hand made no contact. It simply slid right through him with no sensation at all. She was the one without substance, something she never had when she was in this state of hovering. Contact was out of the question.

"You're dead right about your mother," Sam murmured.

She pushed her hands behind her back, hiding

them in the folds of the white dress she was wearing before she acted foolishly again, and concentrated on her status. She was a fairy godmother. Someone who made things possible for humans, who nudged and prodded and plotted to help humans find that perfect love that just about every one of them seemed bent on missing.

"Let's get the hell out of here," Dennis said as he turned abruptly and headed for the door.

He moved so quickly, she didn't realize what was going to happen until it was over and done. He moved right through her and then stopped. She turned, stunned that she hadn't known his intentions before it happened. She was startled to find him apparently looking right at her, and for a heart-stopping second, she thought the shock of the last moment had made her materialize without realizing it.

She'd done that twice lately, both times in Dennis's house, but it took one look down to know she wasn't visible, in human terms now. Yet Dennis stared right where she hovered and he frowned.

"Did you catch that scent?" he asked.

Scent?

"What scent?" Sam asked as he opened the door. "All I smell is the enticing fragrance of Audry's air freshener mixed with toner from the copier." He looked back at Dennis. "What is it?"

"For a minute, it was like a meadow...flowers..." He inhaled, then shook his head sharply. "You're right, toner." He turned and followed Sam out, just taking the time to snap off the overhead light before closing the door behind them.

Angelina drifted back and up, barely hearing the

outer door open and close before she drew farther away, with every intention of heading back to her current assignment. The job wasn't one of her favorites, involving two people who were being particularly truculent at the moment. But she'd left them in a romantic Jacuzzi at a resort in Big Sur with a bottle of vintage champagne. It had been her observation that two people, naked, in a hot tub, drinking champagne, rarely fought.

She drifted off, her last glimpse of Dennis in a large black automobile that looked to be half truck and half car, driving out of the parking garage following Sam's car. At the last minute, before she nodded off to Big Sur, she took a detour to the Benning mansion in the hills of Santa Barbara.

She hovered until she found Emily Benning lying on the chaise longue in her sitting room, a cool rag on her forehead and her eyes closed. She appeared tiny and delicate and pale. But from the looks of her husband, Dennis Benning, Senior, standing over her, he wasn't seeing her in the same way.

"Emily, enough is enough. You can't change Dennis. He is bent on doing what he wants, and, truthfully, he's well past the age where he needs our consent to date anyone." The older man narrowed blue eyes that mirrored both his sons'. "He's doing a damn fine job with his life. Leave him alone."

Emily's tiny mouth drew into a very displeased line. "It's your doing, you know. You're the one who had a...a youthful, and very ill-advised, indiscretion."

"I said that's enough. You're speaking about my son."

Her eyes opened, but she didn't move. "We have one son, Dennis."

He exhaled with exasperation, his hands closed into fists at his side. "Enough. Do you hear me? Sam is my son. Dennis is my son."

"Oh, please," she breathed with a futile wave of her small hand into the air. "Stop."

"You stop. I have had enough of this attitude from you."

Angelina knew with a certainty that there was no love between these two, and maybe there never had been. She only knew what Miss Victoria, her superior, had told her about the Bennings. But even if the marriage had been less than passionate at the first, didn't human love grow and develop?

Emily sighed heavily, as if she were the one put upon. "Attitude. My dear, I am not the one who opened our home to that man."

Dennis Benning appeared almost sad as he looked down at his wife of thirty-five years. "How could I not?" he asked.

The idea that this woman was Dennis's mother, produced a strange blur of sensations in Angelina. She couldn't identify any of them but one. Sadness.

She'd been so right back in Dennis's office. When a fairy godmother started experiencing emotions that were not appropriate for this business, it was time to step back and regroup. She shook her head. She didn't want to be involved with any of this anymore, or any human beings at the moment.

"I...feel quite...poorly," Emily whispered. Angelina glanced at the pale, forlorn-looking woman in the chair. "Quite poorly," she repeated in that quavery voice as she pressed one hand to her forehead.

She glanced at Dennis Benning, and could literally feel him withdrawing emotionally from his wife. Whoever had permitted this union had done an horrendous job. Even that stupid cherub that humans had manufactured in fables could have done better with an errant aim of his arrow.

What an idea—a fat little guy in diapers zapping arrows at humans. Too bad it was just a fable, because it would have been so simple right then to just shoot both of the Bennings. She lifted her hands and mimicked the action of aiming an arrow at them. Yes, the idea of shooting those two was very appealing, indeed. Especially Emily Benning.

"Twang! Twang!" she muttered, as she made believe she let the arrows go to find their mark right in their hearts…if they had any hearts left in them.

"Angelina!"

She heard the echo of her name from a great distance, and before she could turn toward the sound, she was being drawn back and away from the humans. The next instant she was at headquarters, but in an area she didn't recognize. Then she spotted the table. Round, glass, seemingly floating in midair, all surrounded by blank, shimmering walls. Slivers of light, circled the middle area with silent beauty. An area she'd never entered before, the Council space.

But there was none of the Council in residence, just Miss Victoria, her superior, a gray-haired woman in a long blue gown and eyelet apron. She was soft and round, with translucent skin and pale blue eyes behind gold-rimmed spectacles perched on a tiny nose.

"Ma'am?" she asked as she took a step nearer the tiny woman standing by the edge of the table.

Miss Victoria's lips pursed and her blue eyes narrowed inquisitively. "Twang? What is *twang,* Angelina?"

She'd seen and heard. Angelina should have known. A slight heat rose in her face and she clasped her hands in front of her. She hadn't felt this nervous since...since that moment when Miss Victoria had told her that Dennis and Melanie Clark would marry and be "comfortable." That had been unacceptable, and she'd proven that it had been. Melanie had found Sam, not Dennis.

But that was in the past. She had no reason to be nervous now, even if she was in the Council space, a place her sort only came when they were in dire trouble. Surely pretending to shoot humans wasn't a crime? "Ma'am, it's a sound effect when an arrow is shot from a bow."

The tiny woman looked totally confused. "An arrow?"

"Cupid, Ma'am, the icon humans use for Valentine's Day. The fat little guy in diapers who goes around shooting arrows into people, making them love each other no matter what. You know the fable. I was just thinking that Dennis Benning's parents should be shot...." Her face grew hotter when she remembered her anger at the two humans, anger that came more easily to her lately than it ever had before. "Shot by Cupid, of course, Ma'am."

Miss Victoria waved that foolishness aside with

one hand and crinkled her nose. "Let humans believe what they wish to believe if it makes them feel better."

"Oh, yes, Ma'am," Angelina murmured, relieved.

Miss Victoria frowned slightly. "Benning?" she asked. "You mentioned the Bennings? What were you doing in their space?"

She couldn't explain that to herself much less to this woman who could never be fooled by a lame excuse. "I don't really know," she said honestly. "I guess I was checking to see how things were going for...for all of them."

"But that is not your concern, my dear. Mary has that assignment, not you."

"Mary?" she asked.

"Yes, Mary, who, by the way, is doing a wonderful job. She is a very fine administrator of our goals," Miss Victoria murmured. "One to be emulated by others."

"Yes, Ma'am," Angelina murmured, hoping against hope that her real feelings about Mary wouldn't surface too clearly right then. Mary was prissy. That was the only word Angelina could come up with for her. She had a way of being ingratiatingly perfect that rankled Angelina in more ways than one.

And Mary was the only one who ever called Angelina Angie, a name Angelina hated. Even still, she had to admit that Mary could probably handle one of the Clark sisters just fine. Those sisters were so easy to like.

"We did not ask you here to speak of Mary or the Bennings or the Clarks." Miss Victoria took a step closer to Angelina and her voice dropped just a bit.

"My dear, we have something very serious to discuss with you, very serious indeed. But we are at a loss how to say this. Your last assignment—"

"Oh," she breathed, the hot tub. "Ma'am, I need to get right back there. I have this couple, the Warren-Smith connection, and I—"

"No," Miss Victoria said sharply. "That is not our concern. We have already dispatched Faith to take over for you there." Her tiny nose crinkled ever so slightly. "And just in time, we might add. That man poured soap onto her and bubbles were everywhere."

"What?"

"They were fighting when Faith found them. Well," she said with a dramatic sigh, "we are satisfied it is under control...now."

"I do apologize. I really thought that if the two of them were caught in the Jacuzzi and had no options open to them, they'd stop being so stupid and—"

"Angelina. What we need to talk about right now, is you." She folded her hands in front of her on the starched apron. "The Council has reached a decision that you have obviously become jaded by this work. You have wandered from your focus, from your mandate, if you will."

"Oh, Ma'am, I know that I haven't been totally focused recently. But humans are so difficult to deal with. They have it easy, just to make a life and find the right person to share it with, I mean, it's a no-brainer, as humans say. Yet they manage to make everything so complicated."

"Well, that is exactly why the Council has decided that you need to take a step back and remember what this is all about. Remember just what humans are, how they live and what they have to deal with every day of their lives.''

She was horrified at what she thought was coming. ''Oh, Ma'am, no, I don't need a refresher course at the Academy.'' Anything but those classes and sessions and therapy and those interactive virtual reality machines. ''I really don't.''

''We agree that it would serve no purpose to put you through that at this time. This goes well past a mere refresher course. We have something quite different in mind for you.''

Angelina was stunned. There was only one other option for unsatisfactory work. Banishment. They were talking about the unthinkable. Despite the fact that this business was getting to her, the last thing she wanted was banishment. How would she survive doing book work and making appointments for the Council? And making all that tea with honey? The thoughts made her shudder.

''Ma'am, I've had a good record since the beginning—service and dedication, with no real failures. If I'm short with the humans right now, well, it's just things…they've been difficult. The last assignment almost fell apart, and Dennis Benning was—''

''That is it exactly.'' Miss Victoria took a deep breath, swelling her ample bosom under the fine blue material. Then she uttered tightly, ''Your problem is Dennis Benning, and humans like him.''

Angelina almost found herself saying, there were no other humans like Dennis, but she bit her lip hard to keep the words inside. ''My problem?'' she asked in a small voice.

"Angelina, we believe that you have lost that ability inherent in our kind to understand humans and their peculiarities. So, it has been decreed that for one week, you must live as a mortal."

Angelina knew her mouth dropped, but she couldn't stop it, no more than she could stop the words bursting out, "You have to be kidding!"

"*Angelina!*" The voice boomed overhead, surrounding Angelina, and she slapped her hand over her mouth to keep a startled scream inside. "*That is enough!*" the voice thundered around her. "*We have spoken!*"

Angelina looked upward into shimmering nothingness.

"*One week,*" the voice pronounced. "*Seven days in human time. Then, and only then will your future here be decided. Is that understood?*"

She kept her hand firmly over her mouth and nodded quickly.

"*You will be under observation to make sure you do everything the way you should do it. Is that understood?*"

She nodded again, slowly lowering her hand as the proclamation finally filtered through. She had to be a human for a week? That was her punishment? That wasn't all bad. It actually seemed tame compared to what she'd thought was about to come.

She stood a bit straighter. Yes, she could do it, as humans said, standing on her head.

"*Pride is not a very attractive trait,*" the voice admonished her.

Angelina flinched just a bit. "No, it isn't."

"*Ah, a lesson already learned,*" the voice said.

"Now it is time for the rules. You will live without any aids, any powers that you possess here. You will live day by day with no hint of what is to come a second before it happens. In short, you will live as a human being."

"What if I need something?" she managed to ask.

"Miss Victoria will be there for you if there is a problem, but she will not intervene on your behalf. Is that understood?"

Angelina nodded.

"Everything else is set for you. You shall participate fully in life, experience every human emotion, feel what humans feel and learn about what they endure."

"Okay. That's understood. But one thing?"

"Yes?"

"They have places to stay, material things."

Miss Victoria waved her hand a bit impatiently. "That is all arranged. There is a place provided for you. A position for you, and—"

"Position?"

Miss Victoria nodded. "Humans all have jobs."

A job? They couldn't mean that she had to work while she was there? It had to be a joke. But the thought was barely formed before she could tell from the look on Miss Victoria's face that this was no joke. "You mean, work?"

"Exactly."

"But all I've ever done is...is...this," she said weakly.

"My dear, you have done many things in the process of accomplishing your objectives in this service. Now, it is time for you to be going."

She knew better than to argue any of this. It wasn't negotiable. "Okay, I'll get my things, and I'll be ready to leave in—"

Her words were cut short when she felt herself being pulled back and away from headquarters. "Everything you need shall become clear to you, and the time for your departure is now. It is time for you to decide your destiny."

"Me?" she asked as she was pulled farther and farther from everything she knew and understood.

She didn't even have time to ask where she was going to be sent to be a human, just time enough for one last glimpse of Miss Victoria waving to her and her tiny mouth forming the words, "Good luck."

Chapter Two

"You have a job to do, so get on with it."

The low male voice right behind her startled Angelina almost as much as she was startled by the place in which she had materialized in the real world.

She knew where she was immediately, the city and the exact spot, and it was the last location she thought she would have been sent. A hand touched her, a cold, heavy sensation on her shoulder, and she turned quickly to face a man in the reception area of one of the nicest restaurants in Santa Barbara, California.

She was fully materialized and could be seen by humans.

That was obvious. The man in front of her, tall, thin, in a full tuxedo with a bloodred rose at the lapel, was frowning at her. He studied her with barely controlled impatience. "Well, are you ready to work or not?"

"Work?" This was wrong, very wrong.

He took a half step toward her, making her feel decidedly claustrophobic. "As in do the job that you hired on to do this afternoon."

She would have backed away, to keep some distance between herself and this human, but the heavy antique desk was right behind her. She pressed her hips against the carved wooden edge and tried to think. She couldn't begin to understand why the Council had sent her here, no more than she could figure out who this human was and why he thought he had the right to tell her what to do.

"He is your boss, Angelina," a voice said inside her, the voice of Miss Victoria. *"You are what humans call a hostess, a person who greets diners. A pleasant position, I believe."*

As Miss Victoria gave her information, Angelina saw herself in a mirror that hung by the door at the opulent entry of the restaurant. The gilt-framed mirror reflected an image that only added to her confusion. Her curly hair was done in a way she'd never considered before, all caught at the top of her head and fastened with a sparkling clip. But her dress was something she knew and knew well. It just shocked her that the Council had condoned her wearing it again.

It was black and long and clinging, and the same dress she'd worn when she'd been here before, pretending to be the hostess when she was working on one of the Clark sisters' cases. Reggie's case, to be specific. But now a red rose, the only color in the outfit, was pinned by her heart.

If only the Council had asked her about where to go for this week, she would have suggested Hawaii or Bali, or maybe the French Riviera. Not Santa Barbara, and not this restaurant. This decision of theirs made little sense to her, especially when Miss Victoria had very clearly told her that the Clarks and the Bennings were none of her business.

"I don't understand," she whispered.

"What don't you understand?" asked the man who all but pinned her against the desk. She didn't like him, not one bit, even if he was her boss, and she acted instinctively, nodding her head to zap herself out of there. But nothing happened. She was still there, blocked by the man, and with a vague sensation of discomfort in her stomach and throat.

"This, this job," she managed to gasp.

"I really thought Marian would have briefed you on your duties as a hostess when she hired you," he said.

Her disorientation was settling a bit, and as it did, she began to focus. "Mr....er..."

"Summers."

"Mr. Summers," she said firmly, and was thankful when he moved back a step so she could breathe again. "What are my duties?"

He tugged at the front of his tuxedo jacket. "You are to greet the guests, show them to their tables, and do whatever is necessary to make them feel they are getting their money's worth at La Domaine. They are to feel as if they are in their own home."

Big spenders got good service, she thought. She'd done this before, many times, filtered into a situation in a restaurant, even as a waitress. She could do this. "Okay."

"And remember, the bottom line is the customers are not only always right, they never, ever make a mistake."

She just hoped that she could assume the role of

being subservient with humans. That would be a
stretch, with all the knowledge she had of their shortcomings, but she could do it. She *would* do it.

"You will experience many, many things," Miss
Victoria said in her head. *"Use those experiences for
your benefit."*

"Do I have a choice?" she muttered.

Summers frowned at her, that stiff expression
deepening. "Not if you want to work at La Domaine."

The man was very uptight, and probably for a
good reason. Humans took their work very seriously.
"Of course, I'll do my job," she said. "That's why
I'm here."

"Good." He flicked at an imaginary piece of lint
on his formal attire. "We expect perfection from our
employees at La Domaine."

"Of course, high standards are to be admired."
She said the right thing, not what she wanted to say,
that if he expected perfection, he'd better not hire
human beings. Perfection wasn't one of their long
suits.

"You are a human," Miss Victoria said. *"Never
forget that."*

As if she could.

"Enough of that," Miss Victoria admonished her.
*"Now, there is what is called a locker in the em-
ployee lounge. Everything you need to know is in
there."*

"Yes, Ma'am," she whispered.

Summers frowned at her. "What are—?"

The entry doors to the restaurant opened, and
Summers turned immediately. "Guests," he said.

Angelina looked past Summers and saw her recent past walk in out of the night. Reggie and Ben, hand in hand, smiling. Behind them came Sam and Melanie. The Clark sisters, and the men they fell in love with...with considerable aid from Angelina. A parade of her past assignments, her victories.

Francine, the third sister, stepped inside. She had the same coloring at the others, dark hair, lovely amber eyes, and the same build, slender and leggy. Pretty by human standards, she thought. Then there was someone else right behind her, and as Angelina saw Dennis come inside, the oddest thing happened.

Simultaneously with her taking in the fact that he'd changed into a dark, well-cut suit worn over a silky white, band-collared shirt, something beyond the undeniable pleasure at seeing him hit her. Something bounced in her chest, giving her a peculiar sensation that she'd never experienced before.

She pressed a hand to the spot by her breastbone, barely missing crushing the rose, to try to still the feeling. Then he looked up, and the bluest eyes were meeting hers, a smile curled his mouth, and the bouncing hit so hard this time that she could feel it against her palm.

It wasn't painful, but it wasn't normal for a human, even she knew that. It made it hard for her to breathe. She'd never thought about breathing until right then. It was a given. Involuntary when she was in human form. But right then, she had to concentrate to pull air into her lungs.

She barely had time to wonder if this was what it felt like to be sick in human terms, before a hand touched her arm, urging her toward the group. Then

Summers was stepping forward, his hand out-stretched to Ben. "Welcome to La Domaine, Doctor Grant." He shook hands with Ben, then Sam, and turned to Dennis. "Mr. Benning, a pleasure, sir. Your reservations were for a party of six at eight, I believe?" He snapped his fingers in Angelina's direction. "Please check that and see where they are assigned."

The group looked at her right then, and in some way she expected something from them. A spark of recognition? A flash of familiarity? After all, she'd been the one to make sure they were here together. But they were looking at her as if she were a stranger. Exactly what she was to them. None of the humans ever remembered seeing her when she materialized.

She tried to smile at them, hoping she looked okay, then she spoke to Summers. "The table, where would that information be?"

He didn't miss a beat or a smile as he approached her and motioned to the desk. "It's on the chart."

The chart? She followed his motion and saw what appeared to be a layout for the restaurant. The Benning name was written over table number twenty-one. "Large table in the private side room beyond the dance floor," Summers whispered for her ears only as he reached around her and picked up several leather folders.

Then he stood back and held out the folders to Angelina. "Show the guests to their table, and provide a complimentary bottle of our finest champagne." He smiled at the group. "*Bon appétit*."

With a flashing look at Angelina, he strode off down a short side hallway to the right.

Angelina braced herself, clutching the folders to her chest as she turned and forced a smile. "This way, please."

She crossed to the main entry, and remembering things from her last visit, she stepped down into the room. She knew where Summers wanted them, in the best semiprivate area of the restaurant. She led the way across the thick Persian carpeting, past discretely positioned tables and the dance floor in a domed-ceilinged turret-shaped area to the left. Couples were dancing to a very soft version of "My Funny Valentine."

She went directly to a side room, through an archway, and up one step into the more private area. An intricate chandelier suspended from a heavily beamed ceiling cast moody light over a leather and tapestry dining set, covered with lace and centered by fresh roses in crystal. Leaded glass windows on the back wall overlooked the ocean and a night sky dusted by stars and touched by a half moon.

As the couples seated themselves, Angelina laid the menus by them, then stood back. They laughed and talked, and she subconsciously sighed with a sense of accomplishment at what she'd managed to achieve with this group.

She amended her thoughts quickly. It wasn't pride, not really, more a real sense of rightness.

"A very lovely picture," she heard Miss Victoria say for her ears only. *"Lovely indeed."*

She nodded in agreement as her gaze skimmed over Ben and Reggie, to Melanie and Sam, then to

Francine.... She hesitated before she looked at Dennis. He sat with his back to the windows, the night offsetting his sandy-haired good looks.

She went closer to the table, wondering why she felt as if she were bracing herself as she got nearer to the humans. Then she knew. Dennis looked up, their eyes met, and he smiled. She all but flinched at the thud that vibrated in her chest. The same as the first time, and not entirely uncomfortable. Just strange. Something she'd have to look into when she had a chance.

Suddenly a strange expression flickered across his face, a flashing moment when she could have sworn he knew her. Then it was gone, and he shook his head ever so slightly. The thud in her chest skipped twice against her ribs and she pressed her hand there.

Thankfully she saw another formally dressed man approach the table. "Good evening, my name is Andrew, and I'll be your server. Our house specialty this evening is poached Alaskan salmon, complimented exquisitely by a delicate dill sauce."

Angelina didn't understand why humans insisted on eating lovely fish, but it obviously appealed to the group if their smiles and nods were any indication of their approval.

"Perhaps you would enjoy some appetizers before ordering?"

Dennis looked at her and that smile was there again. "What do you suggest?" he asked her. "Oysters? Crab?"

The idea of eating any of that for pleasure seemed almost obscene. "Mushrooms," she said quickly, anything to get away from sea life as food.

"Ah, yes, mushrooms," Andrew murmured. "Stuffed with feta cheese. Delicious."

"Mushrooms it is," Dennis murmured, his gaze still on her, and she found that difficulty breathing coming back. She wanted out of there, to a place where she could expand her lungs and take in air without having to concentrate on it.

As the others focused on Andrew with the wine list, she inched backward, wishing she could nod her head and dematerialize. Humans were so very limited, she thought as she moved toward the entry. As she stepped out into the main section, she could still feel Dennis watching her. He couldn't remember her. That wasn't possible. And she had no idea why he stared at her like that. As soon as she could, she turned and hurried back through the restaurant to the reception area.

DENNIS WATCHED the hostess silently move back, and that niggling feeling that he knew her from somewhere just wouldn't die. Since he'd first glimpsed her at the doors, that sensation had lingered, not really growing or defining, but not going away.

Surely if he had known her in the past, he would have never forgotten her. That would be impossible. She wasn't a woman a man could see, then forget.

She had a tall, almost coltish slenderness, interrupted only by high, full breasts and the provocative curve of hips under the clinging fabric of a simple black dress. Rich auburn hair highlighted with flame, was swept back from a perfectly oval face with elegant cheekbones, a delicate chin line and almost porcelain skin. Stunning. A beauty that was almost painful for him look at.

And her eyes, wide and shadowed by improbably long lashes, were a deep, unusual shade of green.

He had to force himself not to stare at the empty archway where she'd just been, and to pay attention to what Sam was saying to him.

"I don't know what I'd do without my business attorney." Sam glanced at Dennis. "You did a hell of a job with Drusen on that contract."

Dennis had never really thought about being a contract attorney, but since he'd agreed to help Sam work out his contracts for his stunt coordination assignments in the movies, he found that he liked the give and take of negotiations. "Drusen was easy," he said as he fingered the chilly dampness of the water goblet to his right. "It was his partner Barrette who fought tooth and nail to get you for eight weeks. I thought a compromise at six weeks was good for both sides."

"Perfect," Sam murmured as the wine steward arrived and began serving champagne. Dennis watched him reach for Melanie's hand and his smile grow deeper as he looked at his wife. "And, hey, Hawaii isn't all bad. A great place for a belated honeymoon, and big bucks. What a combination."

Dennis felt Francine shifting at his side, then she said, "We should all go to Hawaii. It would be so great. Sun, warmth, beaches, nothing to do." She sighed and rested her hand on Dennis's arm. "It sounds like paradise to me."

Reggie laughed at her younger sister. "Well, paradise is going to have to be put on hold for a while, at least until Angel's a bit older.''

"Oh, Reg, the babies would love it. Can you imagine Mikey on the beach? And Angel would probably sleep all the time anyway.''

"Easier said than done," Reggie said, then sipped some champagne. "But we'll take it under advisement.''

Dennis patted Francine's hand. "Let's all think about it, and maybe this summer we can all manage to take a break.''

Francine looked at him, grinning that Clark sister grin that he always loved. "Oh, come on. I thought this was the new improved version of Dennis Benning. That you'd loosened up, that you were practicing spontaneity? Live a little.''

He grinned. at her enthusiasm, so much like her two sisters. "That's just what I thought I was doing.''

"You could still stand a bit more adjusting. We all could.''

Francine was a lovely person, he thought, a woman a man could love completely. But as that thought formed, another came right on its heels, and that second thought stunned him.

Francine was terrific, a woman made to be loved. But in that moment, he knew he was looking at her the way a proud and slightly protective brother would look at a sister he loved. A brother? Dammit, was that what it had been all along?

He looked at the others, Reggie and Melanie, echoes of Francine. He loved the whole damned Clark family. It amazed him, the idea so clear that he wasn't quite sure what to do about it or with it. Or why he'd just realized it at that moment.

"Hey, I was teasing," Francine said a bit uncertainly. "I didn't mean—"

He patted her hand. "Of course. No problem." He glanced at the others again. Why had it taken him so long to figure out something so obvious? This was all about family. He'd wanted a real family, not the sham he lived with his father and his secrets and his mother with her need to control.

It was so simple. And he had it now with Sam marrying Melanie. The Clarks were part of his family. And he loved them for that, every one of them.

"How about dancing?" Francine asked, leaning toward him. Then she was on her feet, tugging at him. "Come on. Quit looking so serious. Let's dance?"

He looked up and smiled at her. "Sure," he said, taking her hand to go out and over to the dance floor. They stepped onto the polished parquet flooring near the musicians, and Francine stepped into his arms. She fit neatly in his hold, resting her head against his chest. Nice and comfortable, very familiar, the way it would feel to dance with a...sister.

Dammit, but he was slow at getting the punch line, he thought as they moved to the music. At least he'd realized it before he got involved with Francine. So far they'd just been friends, good friends, and he liked that. He moved to the music, and realized it was "Dream a Little Dream." He closed his eyes, wondering if there was some sort of plot working against him.

Just hearing the song brought back last night, and

the dreams. And the woman. He moved to the slow music, the dream filtering back, easing into his mind, bringing that woman who drew him like a moth to a flame. He'd had a thought last night, right before he went back to sleep, but he couldn't catch it and remember it.

What he remembered was his feelings in the dream, the totality of his needs and desires. He rested his chin on Francine's head, the images from the dream growing, almost as if he were dreaming it while he was awake. Her close by, her heat, that scent. She was in his arms, he was holding her, and his body tightened, beginning to respond.

He moved back from Francine before she could discover what was happening to him, and as he opened his eyes, he saw her. The hostess. Across the room. Just standing there. Watching him. He stumbled, trampling on Francine's foot in the process, and he drew back. "I sorry," he said quickly, looking at Francine who was smiling up at him impishly.

"That's okay, I've got another foot," she said as the music ended.

He looked back to where the woman had been, but she was gone. "Sorry about that," he said to Francine, and motioned vaguely to their table. "Maybe dancing wasn't such a good idea."

"I think you're weak from hunger," she said as she took his hand and they headed back to the table.

They passed Reggie and Ben going to the dance floor, and when they got to the table, Sam and Melanie were talking quietly to each other. Dennis slipped off his jacket before he sat.

Francine patted his arm almost maternally. "You

have something on your mind, haven't you? Why don't you tell me about it? What are you thinking about?"

He looked at her and knew there was no way he'd tell her about the dreams, or about the hostess. "Work," he said evasively.

She shook her head. "Drink your champagne, and maybe you'll start thinking about more interesting things than work." She lifted her goblet. "Here's to Valentine's Day, and Cupid, and finding that special someone who makes your head spin."

He looked at the archway and into the main dining room, but couldn't see the hostess. Then he turned to Francine and touched his goblet to hers. "Amen," he breathed, and knew he might be closer to fulfilling that toast than he'd ever been in his life.

As SHE CROSSED the main room to take an extra menu to Andrew, Angelina glanced at the dance floor and stopped when she saw Dennis and Francine. Begrudgingly, she had to admit that Mary was doing a great job. Just one look at the way they were dancing, and it didn't take a genius in this business to know things were going right. Eyes closed, holding each other so close, moving as if they were one.

The only unexplainable thing about that moment, was her own feelings. She felt happiness, real happiness that Dennis was finally going to find the life he was meant to have. Yet at the same time there was a twinge of something she hadn't experienced before, but she knew it wasn't a positive thing. It made her stomach flip and her throat tighten.

Before she could figure out what was going on in

inside her, Dennis shifted, his eyes opened, and his gaze met hers. The sudden connection startled her, and she turned with the menu still in her hand and hurried back to the reception desk. She stepped up and out of the main room, rounded the corner and leaned back against the cold wooden frame of the archway.

She held the menu tightly to her middle, took a breath, and needed very much to figure out what just happened. But without a clue where to start. She'd thought blithely that being a human would be easy, but she knew right then that this week wouldn't be easy at all.

"Very perceptive," Miss Victoria whispered. *"Very nicely done."*

She didn't want to learn this way, but before she could respond, someone very human touched her shoulder.

Chapter Three

"What do you think you're doing?"

Angelina turned, and until she saw Summers standing there, she knew she'd thought it was Dennis behind her.

Wondering how some humans could be so distasteful, she simply said, "Just taking a break for a moment."

He flicked the menu with his manicured finger. "That moment could be spent taking this to Andrew. He's still waiting, and so is the customer."

She'd totally forgotten the leather folder she was clutching to her. "Oh, sorry," she said. "I forgot."

"Don't be sorry. Or you can forget this job."

Some humans were such jerks, but she forced a smile. "Of course, sir." Whatever human emotions this man caused her to experience were the most unpleasant things. Not like the other humans she'd dealt with at all. "I'll take it right away."

Before she could move, Summers snatched the menu from her, and reached out as waiter from the bar came past. He took a full glass of red wine from the man's tray, turned to Angelina, and handed her the glass. "Take this to table twenty-five right away, and when you've done that, make a tour of the room, smile, look lovely and focus on the Benning table. They are longtime customers, a doctor, a man with connections in Hollywood and the tall man with his back to the window is the only son of Mr. and Mrs. Dennis Benning, the cream of Santa Barbara society."

She frowned at his description, and he obviously thought the frown came from puzzlement. "Surely you've heard of them? Old money, and *money* is the operative word here. Lots of money and influential friends who also come to La Domaine."

The man smiled and she was certain he would have rubbed his hands together with anticipation if he hadn't been holding the menu. "And when the son takes that big step, it wouldn't hurt if La Domaine was included in the celebration activities."

"The big step?" she asked, really not understanding this time.

"As in wedding. He's been seeing the same woman for a while, and they look very serious. If I'm any judge of character, I'd say we're close to the big day."

So, even this man noticed the connection between Francine and Dennis? "The big day," she echoed. "Yes, of course."

"Now," Summers said, "make yourself useful."

Angelina moved quickly away from him and back into the dining room. She cradled the goblet in both her hands in front of her and headed right for table twenty-five just beyond the alcove where Dennis was dining. She saw another waiter at the table, and when he turned, impatiently motioning her to hurry, she walked quickly toward him.

She passed the dance floor as the string quartet played "Love Is Lovelier," slowly and sensually, and for a moment she was distracted. She looked to her left, wondering if Dennis and Francine were dancing, and ran into something hard and unforgiving, something that sent the wine glass up into the air and threw her backward.

As if in slow motion, she felt herself falling, her arms flailing in a futile effort to keep from hitting the floor. At the same time the red wine came down in a shower, a shower that spread with horrible brilliance on Dennis Benning's white silk shirt.

She hit the floor with a jarring thud, ending up on her bottom, her hands pressed flat to the cold of the parquet flooring. A blur of people surrounded her, then Summers literally stepped over her to get to Dennis. He blotted with a napkin at the white silk drenched in the deep red of the wine, voicing apologies all the while.

Angelina looked up from the hard floor, her body throbbing from the impact with Dennis and the fall, and a feeling of fire in her face. Embarrassment, she reasoned, real embarrassment. Another human emotion she could file away as experienced, an emotion that made her want to just sneak out of the room and make her escape.

But before she could do more than straighten a bit to get leverage to help herself up, a hand was reaching out to her and someone was saying, "I'm so sorry."

She looked up past the strong hand to find Dennis

standing over her. As Summers nervously blotted at the ruined white silk, Dennis shook him off without looking in his direction and came a step closer to Angelina. He hunkered down in front of her, his hand still extended to her and his face filled with concern, but not for himself. For her.

Then she reached out, slipping her hand in his and as his fingers closed around hers, she experienced her first truly human touch. Summers didn't count. Skin on skin, heat mingling with heat, and right then she knew that the pleasure of being human certainly outweighed her embarrassment.

DENNIS MOVED AWAY from the manager and the waiters who had rushed over to help him, all at the expense of ignoring the woman on the floor, who sat on the polished wood, her hair tumbling free of the diamond clip, her green eyes wide and her cheeks stained with high color. Her long dress had hiked up to expose legs that seemed to go on forever, and a single drop of wine dotted her chin. Anger struck him to the core at her co-workers' insensitivity, and the action of holding out his hand to her came as easily as breathing. Something in him wanted to protect this woman, to help her, and a part of him wanted to touch her. To feel that contact.

She hesitated, then put her hand in his. He closed his grip around her slim fingers, felt a slight unsteadiness in her hand, and that vulnerability made his heart lurch. It only intensified a need to do something to make things better for her.

"Mr. Benning, we at La Domaine offer our sincerest apologies for this clumsiness,'' the manager was saying.

Summers was really getting on his nerves, and the man was probably lucky that the hostess's touch was making it distinctly hard for Dennis to focus on anything but the woman he was easing to her feet. She felt light as he tugged her up and as she eased her hand out of his grasp, he almost felt grief at the loss of contact with her.

"Mr. Benning," Summers said. "I can assure you that there is no place at La Domaine for such incompetence." The musicians started playing music again, this time choosing a dreamy version of "You've Got to Give a Little," and the waiters began to filter back to their work.

"We at La Domaine demand the best of our employees," Summers continued, "and this behavior will not be tolerated. Absolutely will not be tolerated. Angelina, I think this is as good a time—"

Angelina? The name fit somehow. And knowing her name only made this little bureaucrat's obvious intention of making her his scapegoat that much more infuriating. "Mr. Summers," he said tightly to shut the man up. "It was an accident. It's over, and there's very little damage done."

"It was all my fault," Angelina said, tugging at the clip, which finally slipped out of her hair. "I walked right into you, sir. I'm so sorry." She grimaced at his ruined shirt. "Oh, goodness," she said as she saw the wine stains. "That's horrible."

"It was I who stepped right out in front of you. It was my fault."

"Nonsense, sir. She was not watching and almost

knocked you down, and your shirt...well..." Summers sighed with obvious censure. "Just inexcusable."

"Yes, inexcusable," she murmured. "I should have been more careful, and..." She unexpectedly reached out and touched the huge wine stain on the front of his shirt.

He felt his breathing catch when her fingers brushed across the stain, to rest lightly just above his heart. "I ruined it. I'm so sorry."

"Mr. Benning, we can go to my office and take care of this to your satisfaction." Summers looked at Angelina. "And you, go and take care of yourself, then get back to work."

Those incredible green eyes of hers flashed to the manager, and for a moment they were filled with annoyance. Dennis waited for the explosion, knowing he was going to enjoy it, but it never came. She lowered her gaze, hiding the fire completely, and bowed her head ever so slightly, almost subserviently.

She wasn't beaten by the man, but she wasn't about to face him down, either. She moved back as Summer touched Dennis on the arm. "This way, sir," the man murmured, and when Angelina started toward the doorway, Dennis followed with Summers.

They stepped up into the reception area, then Summers led the way down the side hallway to an unmarked door at the end. He stepped forward, opened the door and motioned Dennis inside, then turned to look at Angelina standing in the hallway. "Go and clean up, in the lounge, and get back outside," he said.

"The lounge?" she asked.

"There," the man said, pointing somewhere to his left. "And don't dawdle."

The man turned back to Dennis, and swung the door shut. As soon as the barrier was in place, Dennis felt a sense of loss. It had nothing to do with the ruined shirt he knew he'd have to throw away. It had everything to do with Angelina.

ANGELINA WATCHED the door swing shut, closing out any sight of Dennis, then she rubbed at the soreness in her bottom. She'd fallen. She'd experienced a bit of pain when she'd materialized before on assignments, a stubbed toe, or the time that drunk had accidentally thrown beer on her and stung her eyes. But nothing like this. She'd never experienced hitting a human, or striking the floor with her bottom and hands.

Another experience to file away, along with the disgust with Summers. The man was so horrible, someone not even humans should have to endure. In contrast there'd been that moment when she'd touched Dennis's shirt and literally felt his heart beating under the ruined fabric.

She lifted her hand and stared at the tips of her fingers. A human heart. She'd touched it. The thought was so incredible that her hand was a bit unsteady. The center of human emotions, and their thread that tied them to life. Awesome. She pressed her hand to her own chest, felt a beat, and knew that the lurch in her chest had been her own heart.

Did every human have that happen? That blip that caught your attention? That sudden thud when you least expected it? She'd never heard of it before, but now she'd experienced it. She turned and slowly walked away from the office to find the lounge Summers had mentioned. She neared the rest rooms and a small alcove by the doors where three pay phones sat above a marble shelf.

Not only could she feel her heart beating, but her legs felt oddly unsteady. She moved to lean against the side wall of the alcove for support. There was so much to experience, and those sensations always seemed to overlap one another. Nothing came in single doses for human beings. Not even running into another human being and spraying wine all over him.

She felt so foolish, the embarrassment lingering long after she thought that it should. It was over, yet she couldn't stop thinking about what she should have done. She should have been watching where she was going, watching for diners, been aware of what she was doing.

"Humans call that second-guessing," Miss Victoria's voice said suddenly, startling Angelina. *"It does no good, my dear. No good at all. What is done, is done."*

She was right, but that didn't lessen her sense of...what? What was it that wouldn't let go of what had happened?

"Guilt—human guilt," Miss Victoria sighed. *"It has been known to start wars and end lives."*

"Nothing that serious," Angelina whispered.

"No, of course not. Just realize that humans make mistakes all the time. And you are human."

"But I'm not." Angelina opened her eyes and

looked up at the ceiling in the alcove, wishing she were with the tiny lady right now.

"As long as you are there, you are very human, very human indeed. With all the foibles and all the shortcomings that can entail."

That was the trouble. "I would be doing a better job of this if I had been given time to prepare," she said.

"Humans have no chance to prepare for life. They just live it, day by day, moment by moment. And you are to live this week with only the tools that they possess. You are a human being for now."

Boy, was she ever, she thought. "I know." One week wasn't much time when you thought of it in human terms. Seven days. And she had materialized in this world before. This was different, no nod of the head and dematerializing, but she was smarter than most and could figure this out.

"Do not underestimate the intelligence of humans," Miss Victoria said. *"Not all of them are weak and self-centered like your Mr. Summers."*

"He's not 'my' Mr. Summers," Angelina said, cringing at the thought. "The man is so annoying, and when this is over, I think something should be done about him." Turning him into a toad would do nicely, she thought.

"Angelina!"

"Ma'am, I'm sorry," she said quickly. "Of course, we can't do that. I just meant—"

"We understand what you meant. Just concentrate on yourself and what you need to do. Try not to injure any humans."

The only one she'd come close to injuring was

Dennis, and the word didn't begin to describe his shirt. "Ma'am, do I have money while I'm here?"

"We told you that everything you need is in that locker in the room directly across from you."

She turned and saw a door with a discreet brass plaque labeled, Employees Only. "But I have money?"

"Why are you so preoccupied with money?"

"I have to buy Dennis a new shirt. I mean, it was all my fault that his shirt is ruined. I spilled wine all over it." She closed her hand into a tight fist when she realized she could almost sense his heart beating against her fingers again. "I owe him that much."

"My dear, you have helped Mr. Benning in ways you cannot begin to fathom. You hardly owe him anything. It is he who owes you."

As she turned back to the alcove and closed her eyes, she found herself asking something she'd thought about a lot lately. "He *is* going to be happy, isn't he, Ma'am?"

"It appears so. We are very pleased with the way things are developing in that area." Angelina heard a soft sigh after the words. *"Mary is doing a wonderful job."*

She thought about the look on his face while he was dancing with Francine, and knew enough about humans to recognize that expression. If he wasn't in love, he was indeed fascinated by the woman he'd been focused on at that moment. Finally, Dennis would find the love he needed. Her chest tightened, and she took a deep breath.

"My dear, you appear a bit nervous."

Nervous? Was that what this unsteadiness deep inside her was and what was causing her altered ability to breathe easily? Another human emotion experienced. "I know I'm confused."

"Sad to say, confusion is part of the human condition. Human beings are confused most of their lives." Her voice was growing more and more distant. *"Take care,"* she said and her presence was gone.

Angelina exhaled and muttered, "I hate being a confused human being."

"As opposed to what?"

Angelina heard Dennis speak at the same time she felt the air stir behind her. She inhaled a terribly shaky breath, caught that scent that seemed peculiar to him, then braced herself and turned.

She didn't know if it was nervousness or confusion right then, but whatever human emotion she experienced at the sight of Dennis made her feel terrible. Not being able to breathe properly was bad enough, but her legs were getting more wobbly and her middle was uncomfortable.

She could see that he now wore a dove gray shirt made of fine material that clung to his shoulders and tucked into the waistband of his dark slacks. The neck was open, exposing his throat and a pulse that beat steadily there, an echo of his heartbeat. But nothing like the frantic beat of her own heart at that moment.

Being a human being was a lot more complicated than she'd ever thought it would be.

DENNIS ESCAPED FROM Summers only after agreeing to wear an extra shirt the man kept in his office and to accept restitution from the restaurant. He had closed the door and turned, when he saw Angelina, less than ten feet down the hallway, half visible in the opening of a side alcove to the right. He could hear her talking, but he couldn't see who she was talking to. A woman? A man? Surely a woman like Angelina wasn't alone. There would most certainly be a man somewhere around. What man could be with her for very long and not fall for her? That thought brought a smile to his lips. She'd been the one to fall this time, he'd just been the one to take the brunt of spilled wine. And he'd do it all again if it meant he could get that close to her one more time.

As he got even closer, he could see she was alone.

"I hate being a confused human being," she whispered into thin air in the empty alcove. No man, no woman, no telephone. She was talking to herself, and very emphatically, too.

He instinctively went closer, said, "As opposed to what?" and braced himself as she took a sharp breath, then turned to face him.

Her deep green eyes were wide, and color filled her cheeks again, emphasizing the clarity of her skin. This woman touched something in him that was so intense, it took all of his control to try to act casual.

"I'm sorry. Did you say something?"

"You said you hate being a confused human being. I was just wondering what other options you had?" He sounded silly and he knew it, but he couldn't think of another thing to say right then. Certainly "You're the most beautiful creature, human or not, that I've ever seen" wouldn't be any more appropriate than "Haven't we met somewhere before?'' would be, even though both were absolutely true.

She spread her hands, and he noticed that there were no rings on her long, elegant fingers. "It was just a figure of speech, and I was thinking out loud."

"About what?" he asked.

"About..." She bit her full bottom lip, then blurted out, "My job. I just started and I'm making a mess of things, and I was giving myself a pep talk."

"You're Angelina?"

"Yes."

"That's my niece's name."

For some reason that made her smile, a delicate expression that lit up her face and opened up something deep inside of him. It touched the green depths of her eyes and the increased beauty it brought with it was stunning. In a split second he realized a truth. He'd been missing something all his life, and hadn't even known it existed until now, with this woman. A woman he felt he'd known forever, yet he'd never met her until now.

"Your niece is called Angelina?" she asked, with inexplicable pleasure.

"Yes," he said softly, distracted by his own thoughts right then. "They...they call her Angel."

"Angel?" she whispered.

"You know, like a cherub." He flicked a hand at the mirror in the alcove framed by gilt cherubs. "Cupid."

She crinkled up her nose, but the smile lingered even then. "Oh, so she's a fat little guy in a diaper with a penchant for shooting humans with arrows?"

He laughed at that. "No, she's none of those things. She's beautiful, and sweet, and not a guy, but, I have to admit that she does wear diapers."

She shrugged with the suggestion of a smile. "I'm sorry. That Cupid myth just goes against my grain."

He leaned one shoulder against the wall by the alcove and studied her. "Oh, I get it. You're one of those 'bah humbug' people when it comes to love."

Her green eyes widened. "Me?"

"Yes, you. You probably don't believe in love, or that it even exists. Am I right or what?"

"Boy, are you wrong," she said.

His own smile faltered just a bit. She sounded as if she knew all about love, as if she'd experienced it. It had been stupid to be relieved because there was no ring. That didn't mean there wasn't a man, or that she wasn't in love. "How wrong am I?"

"Very wrong."

"Then you're an expert in the matter?"

That brought another smile that he didn't quite understand. "As close to one as there is."

"Really? What do you have—a degree in love?"

Her bubble of laughter ran riot over his nerves and he wished the sound could be bottled and brought out in the stillness of the night. Dammit, this woman was making him downright poetic.

"No degree, just a lot of—" She broke off her own words and the smile was gone suddenly. "I really need to get back to work."

"Wait," he said, not about to ask her tell him what she had a lot of. He was pretty sure he didn't want to know the answer right now. Instead, he reached out and touched one finger to the spot of wine on her chin. He felt her start, but she didn't move back.

Chapter Four

"Sorry," Dennis said, not sorry at all that he was touching her and feeling the silky heat of her skin as he brushed at the wine spot. "You had a drop of wine there." He rubbed lightly, lingering long after the spot had disappeared, then he finally drew back. "There, it's gone."

She rubbed at the place he'd touched. "Are you sure?"

"All gone," he said.

She drew her hand back and looked at him with great seriousness. "I need something from you."

Mixed with his touch on her, those words brought images to his mind that were more than a bit disturbing. He knew he could find a need in him for this woman, and he wouldn't have to look too far for it. But he managed to say innocuous words. "What is it?"

"Your size. What size do you wear?"

"What does that have to—?"

"Your shirt size. They come in different sizes, don't they?"

"Of course they do, but why—"

"I need to buy you another one after ruining yours, and I have to have the size to do that." Before he could object, she said, "Oh, I know what. I can get your ruined shirt from Summers and match it. That way I can't make a mistake."

"Angelina, you don't have to—"

"Oh, I do. I should. It's what any polite human being would do. And I'm a human being, so—" A low rumbling sound cut off her words, and color deepened in her cheeks as she pressed a hand to her stomach. Her fingers splayed on the delicate black material of her dress. "Oh, my," she breathed, her eyes wide. "Oh, my goodness."

He loved the way she blushed. Absolutely fascinating. "It sounds to me as if you're hungry."

She looked down at her hand on her stomach. "Hungry?" Those green eyes came back to meet his gaze again. "Oh, do you think that's what that horrible noise was?"

"My best guess would be your stomach is rumbling because you haven't had time for dinner."

"Yes, I must be hungry." She looked oddly relieved.

"You don't know when you're hungry?"

Her eyes met his. "Of course I know. Human beings know when they're hungry, don't they?"

"So, we've decided that you're a human being?"

"Of course I am. And I'm hungry. My stomach made noises."

"Exactly."

This was more than an odd segue in their conversation. "Now, since we've decided that you're human and hungry, when can you get a dinner break?"

"Not for a while if she doesn't get back to work right now." Summers was there behind him, talking with that annoyingly tight tone of voice.

"That's my fault. She was too polite to tell me to get lost," he said and saw Angelina assume that subservient tilt of her head. He hated it.

"Well, at least she's being polite," Summers muttered, then added, "I want to make very sure that you understand that this evening is courtesy of La Domaine."

"Oh, yes, I understand," Dennis murmured, wanting nothing more than to see that smile on Angelina's face again.

"So, there you are."

Dennis heard Sam call out to him, and turned as his brother strode down the hallway toward the three of them. He tugged at the front of his shirt. "I needed to make a quick change."

Sam nodded to him, then glanced at Angelina. "You didn't get hurt, did you, Miss?"

Dennis looked back at Angelina as she shook her head. "No, I'm fine. But I ruined his shirt, and—"

"My brother has a closet full of shirts. More than he can wear in this lifetime. One more or less isn't a major catastrophe."

"I like nice shirts," Dennis retorted, hating the fact that the only thing he could focus on right then was the way Angelina's hair brushed against her shoulders. "Did you come to find me to tell everyone about my shirt collection?"

"Of course not. Our food's ready."

Food was the last thing on his mind right then, but

he said, "Great." He looked back at Angelina. "If everything's okay...?"

She nodded, her loose hair caressing her shoulders with the motion. "It's fine."

"Well, have a good evening." He nodded at Summers, then turned from Angelina and started off with Sam.

"I thought the man was going to have a heart attack when you ran into that woman," Sam said on a rough chuckle. "The little twerp. But, if you ask me, it was all your fault."

"I knew I could count on you to defend me," Dennis said as they stepped into the reception area.

"How can I defend you when you hit her like a ton of bricks? Not a good way to meet a beautiful lady, brother."

"Not good, but effective."

"You got her attention." Sam stopped for a moment by the reservation desk and looked at Dennis. "This is odd, and don't you laugh, but I have the strangest feeling I've met her before. I haven't, I'm sure I haven't, but...she must remind me of someone."

Dennis glanced down the hallway where Summers was with Angelina, leaning toward her talking intensely. "You know, I had the same feeling at first," he admitted.

Sam touched his shoulder, but he kept watching Angelina, the way she fiddled with her loose hair, twisting it around and around one forefinger. "I hope you didn't use that line on her," Sam said. "The old 'Haven't we met somewhere before?' drivel?"

From nowhere, Dennis had the flashing image of

Angelina and the beach house that Sam and Melanie had just bought. The darkness of the ocean, night skies. He shook his head, and had no idea where that wild association had come from. Although... night...at the beach...Angelina. Maybe it was just the infinite possibilities those images raised in him.

"Hey, brother?" Sam said, and Dennis tore his gaze away from Angelina. "I was wrong. Mel was wrong. We both thought you and Francine..."

"Where is this all coming from?"

He shrugged. "You aren't in love with her, are you?"

"Of course I love her. I love her. I love Reg and Mel. Hey, I love you. But that doesn't mean I'm *in* love with you."

Sam laughed at that. "Well that's a relief."

"Sam, I love the lot of you, you know that. You're the family I always wanted." He shrugged. "Francine's terrific. She's great."

"But?"

He could barely think straight right now. Every thought was bombarded with Angelina. "Why are you asking me this now?"

"It just hit me when I saw the way you were looking at... I don't know her name. The hostess."

He noticed it and that didn't surprise Dennis. "Her name's Angelina."

"You're kidding? I never heard of an Angelina until Ben and Reggie's baby. Now there's another Angel."

Another angel. Dennis let that thought sink in. "And just how was I looking at her?"

"Let's just say if I thought you were in love with Francine and she loved you, and I came across you in the hallway of a restaurant leaning toward a woman like that and looking at her like that, I'd deck you."

Dennis smiled, not about to deny any of it. "Yeah, sure you would...if you could."

Sam laughed. "Trust me, I could. And if I wasn't so hungry, I'd take you outside and show you just what you had coming."

"And I'd deserve it," he said as he started for the dining room.

THE MOMENT DENNIS and Sam were out of earshot, Summers leaned closer to Angelina and said in a tight voice, "You have had your one warning. If you ever mess up with a guest again, you will not be working at La Domaine. Is that clear?"

Angelina looked into the narrowed eyes of the man and could imagine him with warts and eating flies. A lovely thought. Not that she could really do that to a human, but the idea was appealing. "Yes, very clear," she murmured, trying her best to look dutifully worried about her position.

"Good. As long as you understand." He stood straighter and adjusted the cuffs of his pressed shirt. "Stay away from the Benning table for the rest of the evening. I've assigned Marian to help Andrew with their service." He glanced at her with a slightly distasteful lift of one eyebrow. "And do something with your hair as quickly as possible."

She was more than a bit annoyed that she couldn't

just visualize her hair the way she wanted it to look
and have it done perfectly. "Right away."

"In the employee lounge, not in the powder room.
That is just for guests."

She ducked her head and crossed the hall to the
lounge door, which led to a sterile, cold-looking area.
She hated the whole subservient role some humans
had to assume in life. It certainly went against her
need to control. She closed the door, a bit taken
aback that she'd actually done something humans
were very prone to doing. Analyzing themselves. It
was almost a fad with humans, figuring out why they
acted the way they acted—not that it made them act
any better.

She looked around at white walls lined with gray
lockers and green-tiled floors underfoot. On a ply-
wood shelf beneath a mottled mirror sat a single box
of tissues and a small desk clock that showed it was
ten o'clock already.

Angelina crossed to the mirror, faced with her
slightly distorted image. Her hair was a mess, the
curls falling in wild abandonment around her face.
She leaned closer to take a better look at her chin
where Dennis had touched her. There was no wine
spot left, but the memory of Dennis brushing her skin
was very much still there mixed up with a tumble of
questions.

She touched her chin. Why could one human's
touch be so horrendous when another's could be
so...pleasurable? Summers made her feel weird, a
totally unpleasant experience. But when Dennis had
taken her hand to help her, when he'd touched her
face, the sensation had been vastly different. Her fin-

gers lingered on her chin and the questions were un-
answerable right then.

With a sigh, she stood back and tried to redo her
hair, making some semblance of order from the
chaos. She finally managed to fashion it into a French
twist with only a few stubborn tendrils escaping at
her temples. She knew one thing for sure. Humans
had to work terribly hard to make their hair acceptable, not even perfect. A waste of valuable time, and
effort.

As she glanced at the lockers, she remembered
what Miss Victoria had said about everything she
needed being in one of them. She recognized hers by
its new-looking label—A. Moore. Amour? She
smiled. She never would have thought the Council
had a sense of humor.

*"Humans learn something new every moment of
their existence,"* Miss Victoria murmured to her.

Angelina was only momentarily startled by the in-
trusion. She'd come to expect the elderly woman's
presence in her head. "Yes, Ma'am," she said softly
as she opened the locker and saw a large black purse
and a shawl of some sort. Before she could investi-
gate further, there was a knock on the door.

A dark-haired woman in a modified tuxedo that
the waitresses wore, looked inside. "Summers sent
me to get you. You're needed at the front desk."

Angelina swung the door on the locker shut and
stepped out into the hallway with the woman. "A
party of ten. Old money," the woman added. "Sort
of like Benning. Although, not nearly as gorgeous as
Benning."

Gorgeous? So, she was right that Dennis was ex-

ceptionally good-looking for a human being. This
woman saw it, obviously. "You know the Bennings?" she asked as she fell into step with the
woman to go back down the hallway.

"I've heard some things about him. Old family,
old money, good looks. Who could ask for anything
more?"

Dennis did seem to have everything a woman
wanted. No wonder Mary was having such an easy
time getting him and Francine together. "It wouldn't
take a genius to match him up with someone, would
it?"

"Skill, patience, ingenuity," the waitress said seriously. But when Angelina looked at her, she
smiled. "Now, Summers wants the wine for the rest
of the evening to be in the glass, not on the guests.
Don't worry, sweetie, I hired you. I knew you'd be
perfect for this position."

"You're Marian?"

"You forgot my name already?" she asked as they
got to the reception desk and what looked like a
crowd of customers in formal attire.

Angelina didn't have a clue as to how the Council
had set up a past for her, but this woman had hired
her, or at least thought she did. Mind suggestion, no
doubt. "I'm not good with names," she said.
"Sorry."

"Forget it," Marian replied with a flick of her
hand. "Summers is waiting for you."

Angelina looked at the guests and saw Summers
fawning over a woman with enough diamonds at her
neck and ears to light up a ballroom. He saw her and
actually smiled. "And here she is now, Angelina,

your hostess for the evening.'' He touched Angelina on the arm, a cold, unpleasant contact. ''She is here to serve you.'' He glanced at Angelina. ''The wine list and Andrew,'' he murmured to her, then motioned the guests to follow him.

Angelina watched them step into the dining area, heard the waitress whisper, ''Remember, wine in glasses,'' then Marian followed the group into the dining room.

The next two hours passed in a haze of work and more work for Angelina. By the time the clock struck midnight, the only clearly defined images she retained were of Dennis and the others at their table having a wonderful time. The rest was just a blur of humans needing something, a drink, or a fork, or a napkin or a telephone brought to their tables. And the food that was consumed was more food than she had ever thought anyone could eat in a lifetime.

At midnight, Summers told her she was done. Their bar stayed open until two, but the rest of the restaurant was closing to everything but dancing. She was more than thankful to be able to stop work and have time to figure out where to go from there.

She stepped into the reception area, and leaned against the front desk. Her feet hurt, and she looked down at the simple black heels she'd been provided with. They looked fine, but she had a feeling that any shoes would have produced pain when one had to stand on their feet without the option of going to a quiet place to think and get away from the hustle and bustle of the world.

''Don't forget to punch the time clock. And the

help is not allowed to get a drink in the bar after finishing work.''

"I'll remember that," she said. She was anxious to get away from the man, but needed one more thing before she left. "Mr. Summers, I want to replace Mr. Benning's shirt. But I need the size off of the ruined one.''

He frowned at the mention of Dennis and the wine incident. "I hardly think that is appropriate. I'm quite sure it would be far too expensive for you to replace and goodness knows, he does not need an inferior garment in place of the one you ruined.''

Yes, flies and warts and a cold scummy pond for the man. "I'll get him the exact style and maker," she said.

"Miss Moore, please, I have the shirt in my office and it will be replaced.''

Without giving her the chance to argue, he walked away from her. So, she wouldn't know quality clothes if they bit her in the face? That human was living on borrowed time. Someone with the power, someday would take care of him.

"Revenge is not acceptable," Miss Victoria said.

"I know, I know," Angelina murmured and turned, passed the bar entry and headed back to the lounge and her locker to get her things.

The minute she was in the lounge, she stepped out of her shoes, and breathed a sigh of relief as her feet touched the cold tile floor. Pleasure. A form of it. And simply from taking off shoes and feeling cold tile. She'd file that away, too. She picked up her shoes, then crossed to the locker, set her shoes inside, and picked up the purse.

She took out a slim wallet and was going to go through it, but suddenly felt odd. Her legs were shaking again and her body seemed heavier. Maybe it was a side effect from having to stay in this body without a respite. Whatever it was, it eased as she leaned back against the neighboring locker and looked at the things in the wallet. A driver's license. Driving as in a car? She'd never thought of that until now. She must have a car here, but she couldn't drive it. Although, humans did it all the time. It couldn't be that difficult, she reasoned. She'd seen enough just watching the humans. Start it with a key, pull the handle down and go ahead or back and guide it with the wheel. Sure, she could do that.

She read the license. Angelina Joy Moore, age twenty-eight in earth years. Not too bad, she thought when she saw the photo attached to the license. It looked familiar, then she realized it was the image that Miss Victoria had in her records that kept track of assignments and their outcome. And who the agent was who dealt with the couple.

Below the name was an address, 10 Mockingbird Ridge. It didn't sound familiar, but she could ask where it was. Those places where humans got fuel for their cars always gave directions. She'd find one of those.

She counted two hundred dollars in the wallet, and found a ring with two keys on it. One for the car and one for her home? She fingered a medallion dangling from the ring, a circle with a V and a W in it. Nothing she recognized there, either.

She gathered her belongings and crossed the room to step into the hallway when she heard a familiar laugh and turned to see people by the front doors as they left. Ben, Reggie, Sam, Melanie, Francine... She looked away before Dennis followed them out.

She turned in the other direction and went down to Summers's office. Despite the man's rude comments, she intended to find the size of Dennis's shirt. The office was empty, and she went inside. She barely noticed the opulent furnishings, the antiques, the intricate Persian rug. She saw the shirt on the heavy wooden desk in the center of the room and crossed to it.

She set her things on the desk and reached for the shirt. The fabric was soft and silky and as she drew it closer to her, she had the flashing image of it on Dennis. The way it clung to his shoulders and chest. Without thinking of her actions, she brought the fine fabric to her face and inhaled. Dennis's scent clung to it, a pleasing mixture of freshness and aftershave, mingling with the hint of mellow wine.

She closed her eyes as the essence filtered into her, a unique experience, but as she slowly opened her eyes, she was startled when the office seemed to shimmer and shift. Things took on a surreal look, as if she were starting to float upward. But she couldn't float in this form. Humans never floated, and she was still human.

She held the shirt tightly to her breast and took a deep breath. Maybe she'd forgotten to breathe. That could happen. Things humans took for granted were things she was still getting used to. She took another breath, but instead of growing steadier, she felt lighter and the world shimmered even more.

She didn't understand, but she knew Miss Victoria

would. Her hands gripped Dennis's shirt so tightly they ached, and she looked upward. "Help me," she breathed, then heard her name just before she felt herself start to crumple.

DENNIS STRODE DOWN the hallway to the manager's office. "There's something I need to take care of," he said to Sam. He was going to find Angelina to see if they could go out somewhere and just talk. But he didn't tell Sam that. Instead, he'd hedged with a partial truth. "I need to leave my business card for the manager." A waitress had given him directions, along with the disappointing news that Angelina had gone off duty just fifteen minutes earlier. So much for that plan. Still, he could finish his business with Summers. But when he looked into the office, he was thankful the man was nowhere in sight and the waitress had been wrong.

Angelina hadn't left but was by the desk with her back to him. She held something in her hands, something white that she had raised to her face. He stayed very still just watching her.

He'd had fleeting glimpses of her during the evening as she worked, but she never once approached their table again. Never once look at him. Now and then he thought he caught a delicate perfume in the air, that teasingly evocative scent that brought to mind meadows and flowers and sunshine. Like no perfume he'd ever inhaled before.

God, she was beautiful. Her hair was like rich flame, a brilliant splash of life in the stuffy, overdone office. Since she hadn't left he wasn't going to waste this opportunity that someone or something had dropped in his lap. He took a step toward her, saw her lower what she had in her hands to her chest, shiver slightly and look up above her. He heard a soft, "Help me," then realized that she was crumpling slowly to the floor.

Chapter Five

Dennis called out and got to her just before she would have hit the floor. He dropped to his knees, cradling her in his arms, and the raw fear he'd felt at the sight of her collapsing, eased just a bit when he looked down and realized she wasn't unconscious.

She was pale, her lips slightly parted, and she lay limply in his hold, but her lashes fluttered. Slowly her eyes opened, the green as vivid as he remembered, but her gaze was unfocused, blurred. Then she lifted her hand and he felt the unsteady touch on his cheek. Feathery light, shaky, yet as potent as fire on his skin. "You," she breathed weakly.

"It's me." Her tongue touched her parted lips, a tempting sight. "And it's you," he said. "Almost on the floor. What happened?"

Her fingers trailed to his chin and she answered his question with one of her own. "What am I doing?"

"You passed out. Fainted dead away, or at least collapsed very effectively."

"I did?" She closed her eyes for a long moment before opening them and looking up at him again.

"Why would a human being do something like that?"

"The question is, why would you do that? Are you sick?"

"Sick?" She touched her tongue to her lips again. "How would I be sick?"

"I don't know," he said, noticing how good her color was now, but he didn't move to get her to sit up. A part of him was enjoying cradling her like this. Her heat seeped into him, and that freshness that seemed to surround her was everywhere. "You tell *me* why you'd be sick."

She frowned, drawing a fine line between her green eyes. "Sick," she murmured, "such as...?"

"The flu, measles, food poisoning." He smiled down at her, an easy thing to do when she seemed so seriously considering his words. "Take your choice, but give me an answer."

She was very still just looking at him, then her eyes got wide. "Food! That's it."

"Food poisoning?"

"No, just food." She moved then, breaking their contact, shifting back until she was sitting on the floor, much the same way she had been when he'd collided with her and the wine. "Yes, you figured it out." She grinned at him and got to her knees, gripping the edge of the desk to raise herself to her feet. "Very, very perceptive of you," she murmured. "Food. I'm hungry. I never ate. I guess a human being could pass out, couldn't they, if they got hungry enough?"

"A human being could do just about anything, I suppose," he said, killing the urge to brush at a stray curl by her ear. "The question is, do you pass out a lot?"

"Me? Never. I mean, I breathe and I...I eat and do things that human beings do." She let go of the desk to gesture with her hand, and she gasped when her legs buckled and she pitched forward.

Dennis caught her, and drew her to him. She felt slight as she leaned into him, then her arms went around his waist and she pressed her cheek to his shoulder. "Hey, there," he whispered against her hair. "I think we need to call a doctor."

He didn't know what he expected her to do, but it wasn't to burble with laughter, or tip her head back to look up at him with a smile so brilliant it could outshine the sun. Or her to say, "Oh, no, not a doctor. They don't..." She bit her lip. "I don't need one. I think all I need is food."

Her tongue touched her lips again, taunting him with the moist softness, and Dennis knew a desire to taste those lips that rivaled any need he'd ever known in his life. Her smile faltered, her lips parted softly, and any common sense Dennis had ever possessed was gone.

He dipped his head and found her lips with his. Her soft gasp of dismay was muffled by his mouth, then instead of her drawing back, maybe even slapping him for being so presumptuous, she startled him by coming closer. She opened her mouth, her body melted into his, and Dennis knew what it meant to feel as if he could lose himself in another human being.

ANGELINA KNEW the moment Dennis kissed her why humans were so hopeless in the romance department.

She didn't have a clue what was going to happen until she felt the heat of his breath on her face, he lowered his head, then his mouth covered hers. Soft, hot, gentle, searching. So many impressions flooded through her that she gasped from shock, then she did the unthinkable. She went with it.

Her weakness of moments ago came back full force, but this time she had a hold on Dennis, and her mouth was under his. It seemed so right to get closer and taste him. To feel the sensation of his body against hers, his tongue gently touching her lips, then her teeth. She gasped at the feeling of him so close she felt as if she were part of him.

Part of him? Her? That was madness. That could never be. Yet she wanted it so desperately. Human beings were just plain crazy. And she was as crazy as any of them. Kissing this man, feeling him against her, and wanting more.

When his lips moved against her, trailing a line of fire from her chin to her throat, she tilted her head back in abandonment. Then she froze. She was offering herself to him, letting him kiss her, letting him touch her skin. Her, of all people. No, it was wrong, so terribly wrong. This shouldn't happen, it couldn't happen. Not with this man, especially.

She jerked herself back, emotionally and physically from Dennis, stumbling slightly, and gripping the desk again for support. Her lips throbbed, and she couldn't stop herself from pressing her fingers to her mouth as she stared up at him.

She'd seen that look before in humans, but now the look was turned on her. A burning expression of intensity, and even she understood what it meant. Dennis was as involved as she'd been, maybe more. Dennis, meant for Francine. That thought tore at her. He was destined for Francine Clark. And it didn't matter that his look could make her feel dizzy all over again. Or that she could still taste him on her lips.

"I—I..." she stammered, knowing she'd face a reprimand from Miss Victoria, but until then, she had to stop this right here and now. "You shouldn't have done that." She rubbed at her lips. "You're supposed to..."

"To what?" he asked, his voice low and touched with a degree of roughness.

Be with Francine. Be kissing her like that. "You...you're...a customer," she said lamely and knew that she had experienced a new level of embarrassment this time. And she felt horrible at what she'd allowed.

She turned away from Dennis and wished she could walk out of the room right then. That would stop any more madness that this state of humanity seemed to be filtering into her. But her legs were still a bit wobbly and she knew she'd probably never get out of the room without falling down. So she did the only thing she could. She moved back and sank onto the nearest chair.

She clasped her hands in front of her and stared at them as she asked Dennis, "Why did you come in here?"

"My shirt," he said and she caught movement as he retrieved the shirt where she'd dropped it on the carpeting. She had a glimpse of his hand closing over the fine material, then she closed her eyes.

"I'm really sorry," she murmured, not exactly sure what she regretted more, what she did to his shirt, or the kiss.

"I should be the one to apologize," Dennis said.

"No, don't. You're just human."

"Damn straight I am," he said in a low tone that ran riot over her nerves.

It felt as if the vibration of his voice brushed her skin and it was all she could do not to rub at her arms to stop that sensation. One thing she knew with clarity was she wasn't going to have any more contact with this man. No physical contact at all. That part of her temporary humanity was far too dangerous for her to deal with right now. And if she was nowhere around him, she'd be safe...and he'd be safe from making a terrible mistake.

"Angelina?"

The sound of him saying her name almost made her shiver, but she stopped it by wrapping her arms around herself, hugging tightly and keeping her eyes shut. "What?"

"How about going for something to eat?"

Her eyes flew open and she saw him standing over her. Right then she felt very small and very vulnerable. "No." The single, abrupt word made him frown and she softened it just a bit. She wasn't trying to hurt Dennis, just protect him. "I...can't do that. It's against the rules."

He hesitated for a moment, and she held her breath until he nodded and said, "I need to get going. Are you sure you'll be all right in here?"

"I'll be fine," she said.

"Okay, see you later," he murmured and as she closed her eyes again, she heard him cross the plush carpeting. The door opened and closed softly, and he was gone.

"I hope not," she whispered to the empty room.

She didn't have to open her eyes to feel the emptiness that his absence produced in the room. A human thing, no doubt, this awareness of other humans. Humans didn't have it easy, she conceded to herself.

Now, all she had to do was wait for the other shoe to fall. She sat very still, bracing herself for Miss Victoria…or even worse, the Council, to make contact. But as the minutes dragged by, nothing happened. Surely they saw how foolishly she'd behaved, how disruptive she had been in the Benning-Clark pairing.

After an eternity of prolonged silence, Angelina sighed. Maybe there had been no monitoring when it happened. That was possible, and if that was the case, all she had to do was to never think about the kiss again. She could do that. She had so much to take care of in the days she had down here, that she just wouldn't have time to dwell on a mistake almost made.

Right now, she had to figure out about the food part. Her human body needed it, obviously. But food had always been for pleasure before, not a necessity. Not the way it was with humans. Another thing that just complicated the human existence. More complications than she'd ever thought of before.

"Oh, Angelina," Miss Victoria whispered to her on a sigh. *"We are very, very worried."*

She felt her being sink at the sound, and didn't bother opening her eyes. She knew the tiny woman wasn't anywhere in sight, but she was there. And she wasn't getting away with anything after all. "Worried?" she echoed.

"*My dear, one does not have to be a genius to know that you do not look well. What is wrong with you? We were gone just a moment, then came back. You look very ill indeed.*"

Gone? She tried to block the flash of memories and concentrate on her reprieve. "You weren't here?" she asked hesitantly.

"*We saw you looking so…so pale, and we sense your weariness. This is not just from work. One has to assume that there are other problems.*"

Problems? That seemed an appropriate label for what had happened. But if there was no observer, it wouldn't serve any purpose to bring it out right now. "I think this is the way humans experience tiredness and hunger. They have so many things to cope with. It's so…so confusing."

"*Brava, Angelina, another lesson learned. Humans do the best they can,*" Miss Victoria said. "*Well done.*"

Angelina stood slowly, not wanting for that light-headedness to return. "Ma'am," she said, figuring it would be a good idea to divert this conversation. "I need to eat and rest. What should I do?"

"*Find food and eat.*"

That sounded simple enough. "Yes, Ma'am." She picked up her things and slowly started for the door. "I'll do that. Find food."

She opened the door and stepped out into the quiet

hallway. She'd call a taxi. Tonight wasn't the time to worry about working a car.

"Angelina?" Miss Victoria said, her voice soft as Angelina set her things on the table by the phones and reached for the closest receiver. *"One more thing?"*

"Yes, Ma'am?" she said.

"The kiss?"

The words stopped Angelina's hand on the receiver. It had to be the weariness that had made her think she had that item under control. "Yes, Ma'am?"

"We need an explanation," Miss Victoria said.

There was none. At least none that would make any sense to anyone, least of all Miss Victoria and the Council. "Ma'am, I don't have one. It just happened, and it shouldn't have, and I don't understand any of it."

"Ah, a very human response," Miss Victoria murmured.

"But I am not human," she muttered. "This is make-believe, a time out of time. It isn't my reality."

"Isn't it?" the soft voice asked as it drifted away.

Angelina slowly let go of the phone and touched her fingertips to her lips. There was no reprimand, no punishment, no action. But she couldn't feel relieved. All she could do was hear Miss Victoria's parting words echoing in her head. This couldn't be her reality. It couldn't be.

DENNIS WASN'T AT ALL sure why he went back to the entry of the restaurant, then turned and stepped into the bar instead of leaving. He sat at one of the small tables by the back wall and ordered a whiskey, neat. Maybe that would kill the memory of those lips against his. When the drink came, he cradled it in his hands, then sipped the fiery liquid. But nothing took away the taste of Angelina on his lips and in his mouth.

Dammit all, but the woman struck a chord in him that defied explanation. He'd barely met her. He didn't even know her last name, but he'd held her and kissed her, and he knew that he wanted to do it again. And he wanted more than that. Much more. No woman had ever drawn him this way before, and he was having a hard time figuring it out.

He nursed the drink for a while, then waved off a refill and knew that he had to get going. He had to think, and he couldn't do it here, not when Angelina was just down the hall. He laid money on the table, then made his way to the reception area, dropping the ruined shirt into a brass trash basket on his way out into the night.

It was well past midnight and the air was damp and chilly. The scent of the ocean tinged the air and the sky was brilliant with stars and a partially full moon. The valet approached him, but right then he looked to the side where the parking area was rimmed with large eucalyptus trees and saw her.

It was as if his thoughts had conjured her up. Angelina. Standing alone at the end of the walkway that stepped down into the parking area. Her back was to him, and he had the distinct sensation of repeating himself. Of going up to her in the office, of just looking at her, of her clutching something to her chest. But this time it wasn't the office, and it wasn't his shirt in her hands. It was something dark. This time she wasn't talking to anyone. She was very still, staring off into the distance.

He handed the valet his ticket, then as the boy jogged off to get his car, he went closer to her, taking it as a good omen that she was still here. He'd ask her out again, and this time he wouldn't let a kiss confuse him.

He took another step toward her, but before he could clear his throat to let her know he was there, she turned abruptly. In the shades of moonlight, he couldn't see her eyes, but he didn't miss the way her lips parted slightly. "You again," she breathed.

"Sorry, I didn't mean to startle you," he said, taking another step toward her.

"You didn't. I knew...I mean, I thought someone was there." She hugged the items she held more tightly to her middle. "I sensed someone. Like a human sixth sense, I guess."

"Some humans have that. I don't." He stopped about two feet from her. "I've never had any sort of psychic powers." Although, right then he wished he did. He'd love to know what she was thinking about now. "How about you? Psychic?"

"No, I...I guess I read people fairly well, though."

"Oh, body language and that sort of thing?"

"Humans do that, don't they?"

"Some do." Her body language right then was pretty obvious. Her arms clutched protectively around her, the way she took a half step back without being too obvious about it. "I guess it's an instinct."

She looked behind him. "The others in your party?"

"Gone. They left a while ago."

"The dark-haired woman you were with? She's still here, isn't she?"

"No, she left with her sister and brother-in-law."

She grimaced as if it pained her that Francine had left with Ben and Reggie. "Oh, I see."

"You see what?" he asked.

She shrugged. "Nothing. I just...I mean, I hoped that she didn't..." She sighed. "I thought maybe she..."

"Did anyone ever tell you that it's annoying when you talk in incomplete sentences? It makes it particularly difficult to have an intelligent conversation."

"Sorry, I just thought your girlfriend might have found out about...you know."

"Oh, yes." Light dawned. "You thought she might have found out I kissed you?"

"Well, yes, something like that." She tipped her head slightly to one side as if she were studying him. "Did she?"

"Of course not. Why would I tell her about it?"

"I just thought that a human being would be honest with someone they're...involved with." She shifted and he realized she was barefoot. Her shoes were in her hands with a purse and a wrap.

"Who told you we were involved?"

"I heard things."

The valet was there with his car, parking it at the curb and leaving it idling. He crossed to Dennis. "Your car, sir."

Dennis handed him a tip, thanked him, then looked back at Angelina. "What things have you heard?"

"Just things." She motioned to his car. "Your car's here. Aren't you going to leave?"

He ignored that question. "Do you always believe everything you hear?"

"No, but I saw you with her. You were dancing."

"Yes, we were," he admitted, but that admission brought back the reality of where his thoughts were then. The woman in his dreams and Angelina blurred, until he didn't know where one ended and the other began. That sense of knowing her in the past was overwhelming right then.

"I have to ask you something, and I don't want you to think it's a line or anything, but haven't we met before?"

She was silent for a very long time, then shook her head. "Why would you think that?"

"I don't know. But ever since we met, I've had this feeling that it's not for the first time."

"Do *you* think we've met before?"

"Intellectually, I know we haven't. But there's something else."

"Maybe I remind you of someone?"

The house at the beach. On the bluffs. Night. There was something there, something to do with the house Sam and Melanie bought, the house he'd wanted a couple of months ago, and this woman. But he couldn't sort it out. Confusion was not something he suffered easily, and he persisted. "Where are you from?"

"A lot of places," she said, then looked past him when the lights of a car approached. "Oh, darn," she breathed as the car kept going and made the curve out to the street.

"Expecting someone?" he asked.

"A taxi." She sighed softly. "They're taking forever."

"You don't have a car here?"

"Well, I do, but it's...it's not drivable. I called a taxi from inside, and they said it would be here in fifteen minutes."

He opened his mouth, about to suggest that he could drive her anywhere she wanted to go. But before he could say anything, the doors to the restaurant opened and the dark-haired waitress looked out and called, "Angelina, the cab company just phoned. They're very busy, and they won't be able to have a taxi here for about an hour. Do you still want it to come out?"

Dennis looked at Angelina, then called to the waitress, "Tell them to forget about it. She doesn't need one."

As the waitress ducked back inside, Angelina grabbed him by his forearm. "Why did you do that?" she demanded.

"I've got my car here. I'll take you wherever you want to go."

Her hold on him never eased. "I wanted a taxi and now it's not coming. You had no right—"

"I'm trying to help." He hated her being angry like this. He motioned to his car. "It's here. I'll drive you. You don't have to wait for a taxi."

"I don't take rides from strangers," she said tightly.

"I'm hardly a stranger. You know a lot about me,

down to and including whom I'm dating. And after that kiss..." She released his arm when he mentioned the kiss, but he didn't stop with that. "Stranger just doesn't cut it anymore."

She was very still. "I'll wait for the taxi."

"You'll wait an hour. And it's after midnight already. And you haven't eaten, have you?"

"No, but—"

"And you passed out in there, didn't you?"

"No, not really."

"Close enough, and you're really going to pass out if you have to wait another hour for your ride."

"Then I'll go inside and wait," she said.

Dennis wasn't about to beg her, but something in him wouldn't let go. "Okay, if you won't let me give you a ride, show me your car and I'll try to get it going for you."

"No."

He frowned at her. "I'm not much of a mechanic, but I can figure out the basics of a car."

"Nothing is going to make that car drivable for me...at least, not right now."

"Okay, then let me drive you home."

"Do you ever give up?" she asked with obvious exasperation.

"No, it's not in my makeup, I'm afraid."

He saw her take an unsteady breath, then put one hand against the building. "You really should give up, you know."

"I'll think about it sometime, but not now." She started to say something, then stopped and closed her eyes for a moment. "Are you feeling weak again?" he asked.

"No, I...well, a bit." She opened her eyes, then took a deep breath. "But, I'm not going to pass out."

"You will if you stand here any longer. Just take the ride, okay?"

"Go away. You've got family and people to be with. You shouldn't be here at this time of night harassing me."

She was unbelievable. "Harassing you? Lady, I'm trying to help you."

"I don't need your help," she said, but her voice didn't sound very strong.

The old Dennis Benning would have walked away then, but this version never thought of leaving her there, and he'd be dammed if he'd stand by and wait until she passed out cold.

"I'm probably going to regret this later on," he muttered, then swept a startled Angelina up in his arms.

Chapter Six

Angelina squirmed and twisted, but Dennis strode toward the idling black car with her in his arms. "You let me down right this minute," she insisted and wished her voice sounded stronger so it carried more authority.

This couldn't happen. Miss Victoria and the Council wouldn't be nearly as understanding if they found her near him again. After the last time they were alone, goodness knew what would happen now. And in a small car. Well, not a really small car, but they'd be way too close for far too long. And she didn't trust this humanity at all. Not when him carrying her was setting off alarms right and left. "You just remember this wasn't my idea at all, period."

"Sure, whatever. I forced you to do it."

She cast him a slanting glance. "I wouldn't go that far, but I want it on the record that you insisted."

"Consider it recorded," he said as the valet stepped forward and opened the passenger door for Dennis.

He eased her into the car, then stood back as she shifted to settle on the gray leather seat. The things she'd been carrying tumbled to the floor. "Oh, shoot," she muttered.

When Dennis reached for her belongings and picked them up for her, Angelina cursed herself for being so weak. Another human frailty that was messing up her time down here. Passing out probably would have been a better idea by far than being in this car. But the weakness in her legs and the way her head seemed to spin was unnerving enough to make her sit back while he closed the door for her.

The only good thing was he could find the address for her and save her that bother. But that was a very minor plus considering the circumstances. He walked around through the glow of the headlights to get in the driver's side.

"He made me do this," she whispered. "I didn't want to, but I'm so tired from not having food."

There was no response, then Dennis was getting in the other side and settling behind the wheel.

"Relax," he said as he put the car in gear and headed down the driveway to the street. "I'm taking full responsibility for this, if that makes you feel better. And, on top of that, I'm safe. I'm no psychotic slasher, so you'll get home in one piece."

She bit her lip to stop words that came so easily, words about her knowing he was a good, decent man. But all she said was, "Okay, I concede that. After all, you're a Benning."

When Dennis darted her a quick look, she knew she'd said the wrong thing. Human frailty, or human stupidity had produced those words she should have known better than to say to this man. Whatever it was, she knew she needed to backtrack quickly when

Dennis asked, "What does me being a Benning have to do with anything?"

"I'm sorry. I shouldn't have said that," she replied quickly, straining to see his silhouette in the dimness of the glow from the dash lights. "I know how you feel about that, about being a Benning, about taking advantage of that name, of the family position. I mean—"

The weakness in her body was affecting her brain. That was the only excuse she could find to explain why she was digging a deeper and deeper hole with Dennis. She bit her lip hard to keep more words inside, and she flinched when Dennis slowed the car and turned to her. "What in the hell are you talking about?"

There was no way she should know any of that, and Dennis knew it. She couldn't take back the words, so the best thing she could do was cover them with generalities. "Nothing. I just heard that you'd made a break from your family, from the Benning mold, that's all."

He kept driving, but she didn't miss his harsh exhalation before he asked, "Don't tell me they're writing this all up in one of those tabloids?"

"No, of course not. Why would you think that?"

"I thought you said you weren't from around here, so how else would you hear all that rubbish?"

"So, it's not true?"

"I didn't say it wasn't true. I just can't believe that you'd know that."

"Someone just mentioned a few things, that's all. I'm sorry, and it's all rumors, anyway."

He stopped at the Coast Highway and let the car

idle as he turned toward her. One hand gripped the top of the steering wheel, his other hand rested on the back of her seat. "I want to hear everything you've found out about me, but first, tell me where we're going. I need an address for your house."

"Oh, sure," she said and fumbled in her purse for her wallet. She opened it, but the light was dim and she couldn't make out the address. Abruptly, Dennis flicked on an overhead light, and she blinked at the sudden illumination. "It's 10 Mockingbird Ridge," she read out loud. "I just moved in...."

He nodded and flipped off the overhead light. "Now," he said, "tell me everything you've heard about my family."

"Why don't you tell me about your family then I'll know the truth?"

He pulled onto the highway going south. "First, tell me what lies you've been told."

Angelina watched every move he made driving, how easily he controlled the huge black car, how smoothly he maneuvered down the highway.

"What are you looking at?" Dennis asked.

"Your driving. You're a good driver."

"Is it okay if I take that as a compliment?"

"Sure. I mean it. I used to think driving was a no-brainer, but now..." She watched his hands grip the steering wheel, strong hands, no rings. "I think it's impressive that a human can drive well."

"Are you an impressive driver?"

"Far from it. I'm not much of a driver at all."

"Did your driving have anything to do with your car not working?"

"Everything to do with it," she said honestly.

She realized that she enjoyed the sound of his voice in the confines of the car, the way it mingled with the humming of the tires on the road and a slight wind noise. The combination was almost hypnotic, and she rested her head against the high support of the seat.

She turned a bit to look more at Dennis, at his profile in the dim light from the dash. The man only looked better than before, a bit more relaxed, his hair not quite perfect. The shirt clinging to his shoulders like a second skin. Mr. Perfect the Clark sisters had called him before when he was uptight and precise and bound by the laws of the Benning name. Strange how he'd loosened up and shed the confines of his family, yet he seemed even more perfect now.

"So, what do you do?" she asked, rubbing her cheek against the leather and watching him flex his fingers on the steering wheel.

"I'm a tax attorney-slash-business agent. I've started getting involved in my brother's career. Sam's a stunt coordinator for the movies. I help with contracts and agreements, give him business advice."

"And you like it?"

"Yes, as a matter of fact I do."

"The give and take, the negotiating?"

He darted her another look. "Yes, actually, you're right. It's fascinating. How did you know?"

"You sounded as if you liked it. Maybe it's your calling in life."

"I never thought of that, but it could be." He concentrated on the road ahead of them. "How about you? What's your calling in life?"

"Well, it's not being a hostess at La Domaine," she murmured, picking up the wallet still in her lap. "For that you have to be able to walk and carry wine at the same time. Something I can't seem to do."

Dennis laughed, a wonderful sound that made her smile slightly. "You were doing just fine until I walked right out in front of you."

She had a jarringly clear memory of that moment when they collided, then it all mingled with the kiss. She looked away from Dennis and stared out at the darkness of the ocean as they drove through the night. "I wasn't watching," she said softly. "I need to be more careful...about a lot of things."

She felt the car slow, and as she glanced back at Dennis, she realized that he was pulling off the highway. He made a left turn into the parking lot of what looked like a fast-food restaurant. The garish lights in yellow and red flashed through the night, and he drove toward a sign that read Drive Thru.

"What are you doing?" she asked as she shifted in the seat.

"Food. You're hungry and this is right on the way to your place."

"I just want to get home," she said, sitting up a bit straighter.

"You need to eat. I'll go on record that it's my idea."

"I don't think—"

As he stopped the car by a speaker, a disembodied voice crackled into the night and cut off her words. "Welcome. My name's Mimi. How may I serve you?"

"Give us a minute," Dennis said, then looked at Angelina. "What would you like to eat?"

She knew a place like this wouldn't be serving ambrosia, her absolute favorite when she wanted to indulge her senses with eating. "What do they have?"

"You *are* from out of town, aren't you?" he asked with a smile splashed with the colors from the neon signs overhead.

"Humor me," she said.

"Okay. They have hamburgers made in every way mankind has ever thought about making them and with anything on them you can imagine. Now, how do you want yours?"

"Hamburgers? They're made with meat, aren't they?"

"Dead cows," he said with that grin, joking, but it made her stomach lurch horribly.

"Oh, no, no cows." The idea of eating animals was horrendous to her. It was nothing she'd ever even considered doing in her existence, and tonight wasn't going to be the night to begin. "No, thanks."

"Chicken?"

Easter chicks. No, not that. "Absolutely not."

"I suppose fish is out?"

"You suppose right."

"You need protein to get your blood sugar up."

Blood sugar? Oh, that sounded horrible. "I just need food, that's all, but I don't want to kill anything to get it."

"A vegetarian. And we're at the only place open at this hour, and they happen to serve beef with a little tomato and lettuce added. This poses an interesting problem.''

Vegetables. Yes, she could handle those. "Can't they just leave the meat out of a hamburger and give me the rest?"

"All you'd have would be the bread, tomatoes, lettuce, mayonnaise and pickles. That hardly sounds—"

"That sounds wonderful to me," she said quickly. "I'll take one."

At least he didn't argue with her anymore or insist on protein. "Okay, if you can eat it, I can order it. What about a drink? Soda? Milk? Juice?"

"Milk." She'd heard about milk but never tasted it. "Yes, milk, I think."

"Are you ready to order yet?" that voice said over the speaker.

"Yes, I guess so," he said and gave her the order for a large milk and a hamburger without meat.

The voice on the other end came back on. "Let me see if I have this right. You want a hamburger deluxe, hold the meat?"

"You've got it," he said, then drove forward along a narrow lane to a brightly lit window.

A woman dressed in a bright orange top and odd-looking hat leaned out and smiled at Dennis. "That'll be $3.87."

Money. She'd entirely forgotten about that. She still held her wallet, and she opened it, but before she could take out any money, Dennis had paid the woman. Angelina took out a five-dollar bill from the back of her wallet. "Here."

"No, my treat," he said as he took a large cup

from the woman and, after sticking a plastic straw into the hole in the plastic lid, turned to give the cup to Angelina. "Your milk."

"I need to pay. I know that humans pay for what they get."

He was holding the milk out to her while she held the five-dollar bill out to him. "Humans pay. Correct. But sometimes one human wants to pay for another human. It's called a gift. And humans accept gifts with a nice smile and a thank you, then they take their milk while it's still cold. Okay?"

She didn't want to owe this man any more than she already did. But she knew she had to eat. "You win," she mumbled and pushed the bill back in her wallet, then reached for the milk.

She gripped it, her fingers lacing with his in the process, but he didn't let go of the cup. "I have it," she said, overwhelmingly aware of his touch on her fingers.

"Humans thank humans," he said with a maddening smile.

"Thank you," she said.

"And?"

She froze, the contact with him making her mouth feel dry. "And what?" she managed to ask.

"The nice smile?"

She smiled, and she knew that the expression was tight. But Dennis didn't seem to notice. His own smile flashed in response, then he let her take the milk. The container was cool and damp. "Thank you," she murmured, hesitantly touching the straw to her lips, then drew the liquid up into her mouth.

A cool, smooth substance washed over her tongue,

and when she swallowed, she felt it go all the way down to her middle. "Oh, my," she breathed at the instant pleasure she felt from the creamy liquid. Then she took another sip.

"You like milk, I take it?" Dennis asked.

"It's wonderful."

"If you like that, you must be crazy about chocolate milk."

She looked at Dennis to find him studying her with a quizzical smile. "They put chocolate in this stuff?" she asked, the idea definitely having possibilities. Truffles were one of her favorite indulgences when she wanted oral pleasure.

"They do and sometimes they put ice cream in it with the chocolate and call it a milk shake."

"You're making fun of me, aren't you?" she asked.

"I'd never do that," he said with a crooked smile. "But I've never seen anyone get such pleasure from a simple drink before."

He was right, and she was overreacting. She had to watch that. "I was just very thirsty," she murmured as she sat back with half the milk gone from the cup.

"Obviously," Dennis said. He motioned to the console between them. "You can put that in the holder if you don't mind letting go of it for a while."

She slipped the cup into a circular slot on the side of the console, then sat back with a sigh. "I feel so much better already. Thanks."

"If I'd known milk would do that to you, I would have bought you the whole damned cow."

She fingered the wallet on her lap. "You're joking,

but I always thought cows were lovely creatures. I can't think why people would want to eat them. At least nothing was killed to give me milk," she said.

"True, no cows died. I concede that point."

"Exactly," she murmured. She was feeling better and better, that odd fuzziness in her head clearing, and she could feel herself relaxing a bit. "You know, they're really quite lovely animals. Have you ever noticed their eyelashes? They just sweep up and curl and—"

"A cow has eyelashes?" Dennis said, with gentle teasing in his voice.

This human thing was a bit easier now. Dennis smiled. She smiled. Dennis teased her. She enjoyed it. Her reactions were settling down considerably, and she was starting to feel as if she were in control again. A great relief for her.

"Of course they do," she confirmed. "And huge brown eyes."

"I'll have to check it out the next time I run across one."

Her relief was abruptly shattered when Dennis leaned toward her and touched her lips with the tip of his finger. The simple action stripped away any control she thought she had, and when his fingers moved lightly over her skin, she knew she'd fallen into a trap formed from pride.

She'd let herself into this situation, had the nerve to think she could control it and get out of it unscathed. Miss Victoria and the Council frowned on pride, and now she knew why. When a human's touch could do this to her, how could any human think they were immune to it?

THE NEED IN DENNIS to touch Angelina never seemed to diminish. Not even when she was talking nonsense about cows and their eyelashes. It just grew, and when he impulsively touched her lips, the pleasure the slight contact gave him was beyond understanding. He barely knew her, and there was so much to learn about her, yet he thought he knew the most important things.

The way she smiled, the green depths of her eyes, her fanatical love for milk, and a crazy thing, that she made him think of meadows and flowers and possibilities instead of reality. He ran a finger over her lower lip and felt her tremble. "Shhh, I think you need food. You're starting to sound like a PR person for cows."

"Food, yes, I need food," she whispered and moved back just enough to break their contact.

"Sir?"

He turned away from Angelina to the woman in the window. She was holding a bag out to him. "Your order, sir. One deluxe hamburger, hold the meat," she said with a smile.

Dennis took the bag from her and handed it to Angelina as he paraphrased the woman. "One deluxe hamburger, hold the cow."

"Thank you very much," she said as she took the bag, then she smiled. "And notice the smile."

How could he not notice it when it set his world on its ear? "Great, great, now you've got it," he said, hearing a slight unsteadiness in his voice. "Perfect," he murmured as he put the car in gear.

As he drove back to the highway, he heard the rustling of paper as Angelina opened the bag, then there was silence for a moment before she mumbled, "Fantastic. This is better than ambrosia."

"Ambrosia?" he asked, taking the chance of turning to look at her.

She was in the process of taking another bite, and the obvious pleasure on her face was breathtaking. If something as simple as a sandwich brought such enjoyment to her face, what would she look like if she was being made love to? His foot on the gas jerked slightly, making the car lurch, and he blocked those thoughts as quickly as he could.

"Yes, ambrosia. You know, a food fit for the gods. All fruit and cream and honey. Mmm, but this is every bit as good." He could sense her reaching for her milk, then she sighed softly. "Eating is wonderful."

"A veritable sensory pleasure?" he murmured, thinking of much better sensory pleasures that taunted him while Angelina was so close to him.

"Exactly. That's what it should be. A pleasure, not a necessity."

"Another human obsessed with food," Dennis said.

He heard the paper rustle again, then she sat back in her seat with another sigh. "Feeling better now?" he asked.

"Much."

"Better than standing outside La Domaine waiting for a taxi?"

"Of course."

"And...? This is the place where you say, 'Dennis, you were right. I needed to be made to leave La

Domaine and come with you.' And then I say, 'Glad to do it,' and we're both better for it.''

"You're going to have to write this all down for me. I'll never remember your human rules, all the 'Thank yous' and the smiles and never refusing a gift and now this saying you were right." The paper rustled again. "This gets so confusing."

"And you hate being a confused human being?"

He was surprised by a soft chuckle, broken off by a yawn. "Yes, I do," she said in a muffled voice.

He looked at her, her head resting against the back of the seat and her eyes slowly closing. "It's been a long night, hasn't it?" he said as he returned his gaze to the road.

"Yes, very long," she agreed. There was silence for about a mile before she murmured from the shadows. "Tell me about yourself."

He downshifted as they neared the main business section lined by closed stores on one side and rolling grass that went to the beach on the other. "There isn't much to tell. Besides, you were going to tell me what you heard about me. Now's a good time."

She exhaled softly. "Okay. Let me think. You found a half brother last Christmas, Sam, I think he's named. You are very involved with a large family in town, the Clarks. All kinds of kids."

"Nine," he said.

"Yes, that's it. You've dated some of the sisters, and your brother married one of the sisters you dated."

"That sounds decadent, don't you think?"

"Complicated is more like it," she murmured. "But you're very close to your brother, aren't you?"

"You've got good information so far," he said. "We're close. We didn't even know about each other most of our lives, but it seems as if we've always been brothers."

"Kindred souls?"

"I don't know if I believe in that," he said as he cleared the business district and headed south.

"Believe it, it's true. Souls that are meant to be together in this life. As brothers, sisters, families…lovers."

"Preordained?"

"No, more like, if given the right chances, the right opportunities to intersect in this life, they find their matches." She chuckled softly. "Although, sometimes humans fight it."

"You think human nature is funny?"

"No, more perverse and stubborn than anything. Humans trying to make matches where they shouldn't be, and for all the wrong reasons. I bet you've had a few relationships that you thought should have been right, but weren't, haven't you? Like the Clark sisters?"

Was she a psychic? "A lucky guess, or headlines in the *National Gossip?*"

"I just heard that the lady you were with tonight was one of the Clark sisters."

"Francine? Yes, she is."

"The Clarks are sort of like your family?"

He laughed at that absurdity. "Like the family I'd want, but nothing like my real family. As you've pointed out, I was born a Benning."

"Old money, prestige, power?"

"I guess so," he said with a degree of distaste.

"You don't like being a Benning?"

He spotted the exit from the main road and swung left to drive up the hill. "It isn't a matter of liking or not liking it. It's what I am. But it's not *who* I am."

He felt her stir, as if settling in the leather seats as he looked for Mockingbird Ridge. Then she spoke on a low sigh, "So, who is Dennis Benning?"

Chapter Seven

A year ago Dennis would have had a list for that question. The son of Emily and Dennis Benning, an intricate part of Santa Barbara society, heir to the Benning name and fortune, uptight, rigid, obsessive and a thoroughly annoying person. But now he had a simple answer.

"I'm me," he said. "I don't trade on my name. I live on my own money, and I work hard." He fingered the steering wheel. "I'm living the kind of life I always wanted, but never knew I wanted until a year ago. Not tabloid material, that's for sure."

He spotted Mockingbird Ridge and turned right to drive parallel to the main road below the shallow bluffs. Now he'd met Angelina and he could feel his life taking another detour. One he was anxious to see where it led to. That fanciful thought was stopped when something struck him, and struck him hard. He'd done all the talking, and had never asked the questions he really needed answered.

"I bared my soul," he said with forced lightness. "Now it's your turn. Tell me about your life." He forced out the next words. "Are you married?"

There was no response, and Dennis could feel nervousness clutching at his middle. "Okay, if that's too difficult for you, are you engaged, going with someone? Stop me when I get to the right description."

Nothing.

She was making this way too hard. "Something simple. How about telling me your last name?"

Nothing.

"Angelina, I..." His voice trailed off when he saw her in the soft light. Her eyes were closed, her cheek pressed to the leather of the seat, and her hands resting on her lap. She looked as if she were asleep. "Angelina?" he said softly.

She didn't stir. He stopped at a stop sign, and with no car behind him, he reached for her wallet and carefully slid it out from under her limp hands. He couldn't remember the number at all. He clicked on a light on the bottom of the rearview mirror and looked at Angelina.

The soft beam cast delicate shadows in the car, touching her, exposing the dark arch of lashes on her cheeks, the way her breasts rose and fell slowly with each breath she took. He had to force himself to look away and at the wallet in his hand. He flipped it open and saw her driver's license.

Angelina Joy Moore. Angelina Joy? The exact name of Ben and Reggie's daughter. Another strange coincidence. Twenty-eight years old. The color photo of her was so lifelike it was startling. It sure wasn't like the usual DMV mug shot. Then again, he conceded, maybe it was just the uniqueness of the subject. That could very well be it.

He glanced at the address—10 Mockingbird

Ridge, Unit A—then he closed the wallet. He leaned over, slipped it into her purse, then flipped off the light and drove along Mockingbird Ridge. The area was old, one of the sections the city was refurbishing, trying to keep the feel of the forties and fifties, but updating and remodeling for modern tastes and usage.

He drove slowly, then found 10 Mockingbird Ridge. It wasn't a house, or even apartments, but what appeared to have been an old motor court, a series of small bungalows built around a central area and fronted by a single-story house done in stucco. A wooden sign hung by open metal gates and illuminated by low ground lights read Mockingbird Ridge Court.

Dennis pulled onto the gravel drive that led through the open gates and into the courtyard that had been modernized to include a softly lit swimming pool surrounded by swaying palms and gardens. He saw Unit A immediately on the right, and slipped into the parking slot in front of the porch on the adobe cottage.

He turned off the lights and motor, then shifted in the seat to look at Angelina. Part of him wanted to sit and watch her sleep, but he knew he couldn't spend the whole night just sitting here. He looked around, but the other units and the front house were darkened and the quiet was almost palpable. In her purse, he found a ring with only two keys on it. One had to be for the door to this place.

He got out on his side, went around and opened the car door by Angelina. He hesitated, then reached out and touched her arm. Her skin was warm and soft under his fingers. "Angelina? Love, we're at your place." He shook her gently, but all that accomplished was to have her shift more toward him, sigh and settle her cheek against the gray leather seat again.

In the softness of the moonlight filtering into the car, her face looked almost ethereal, angelic. Her name fit her perfectly. He tried to shake her again, but she didn't respond. Leaving the door open, he turned and headed for the cottage, where he crossed to the door and slipped one of the keys into the lock. The door quietly clicked open.

He faced shadows, then felt on the wall to his right, found a switch and flipped it. A small, overhead light flashed on and bathed a combination living and kitchen area in a yellow glow. A bar with a pair of stools cut the space in two, with wicker furniture on the front side, and old appliances and a series of cupboards with a small refrigerator on the back side.

Just past the kitchen, he could see a short hallway. He walked across the hardwood floors, saw two doors and opened the first. It was a small bathroom with a claw-foot tub and pedestal sink. He closed the door, then opened the other. It was a bedroom bathed in the pale glow of moonlight that drifted in through a single French door at the back of the room that lead to a tiny patio area.

The bed with its brass headboard seemed small to him. A dresser stood to the right, an armoire right next to it and a single chair sat by the door. He glanced quickly, but didn't see anything personal in the place. No pictures, no clothes anywhere, nothing out of place at all. No evidence that anyone really lived here.

Yet that delicate scent that clung to Angelina was everywhere, permeating the small rooms and bringing those images to his mind. Meadows and sun and summer days filled with flowers and joy. How could a perfume do that to a person?

He shook his head, and left the room to go back out into the cool February night. Angelina was right where he'd left her. She hadn't moved. He went closer to her. "Angelina, you're home. Angelina?"

She moved a bit closer to the door, her cheek pressed to the leather, but her eyes never opened. He bent down closer to her and whispered, "Wake up. You're home, Angelina."

A slow smile touched her lips, a seductive expression, yet she didn't waken. She just seemed to settle deeper into her sleep. So, for the second time in an hour, Dennis lifted Angelina into his arms and carried her through the night.

But this time there was no fighting and squirming. She settled into his hold, pressed her face into his chest, and rested one hand on his heart. He felt her body tremble with a peaceful sigh, but its effect on him was anything but peaceful. It was a mistake for him to hold her like this again, to be carrying her, to be inhaling her provocative scent, to be feeling her heat seeping into his body.

He got to the door, stepped inside and moved through the softly lit room and into the bedroom. The moonlight cast velvety shadows, and as he approached the bed, he had the distinct feeling of going where he'd never gone before. Not physically, but in a way he couldn't begin to define.

He eased her down onto the comforter, then braced his weight over her with both hands pressed on the cool linen. He looked down at her, at beauty that riveted him, and when she shifted, her face turning toward him and her arms twining around his neck, he didn't try to stop what he knew had to come next.

ANGELINA KNEW she was asleep. Though she'd never slept before, that was what had to be happening. But she never guessed that the dreams she'd only heard about could be like this.

She could feel everything in the dream. Dennis was there, carrying her, then she was drifting down, and she went with her feelings, blotting out any sense of guilt. Dreams were free. They were uncontrollable. She couldn't stop them.

Dennis leaned over her, just like all the humans she'd observed over aeons past. When lovers were on the brink of making that commitment to each other. But in this dream it was her and Dennis. He was there, his body close, then she knew what came next. She lifted her face for his kiss. A kiss that had the power to make her yearn toward him, to hold more tightly to him, a kiss that brought his body against hers.

The Council had said to experience human emotions, and it was safe to experience them in this state called dreaming. She tasted Dennis, arching toward him, feeling a need for him to be even closer, and relishing his weight on her.

All she regretted was she didn't have the ability

to settle in him, the way she could have before. That ability to dissolve and slip through a person, slowly, easily, sensing their thoughts and their needs. Not the jarring way she'd slipped through him at the office when she wanted contact.

She had the contact now, and she'd never known that feeling before. She was in a place she'd only seen before, but never experienced. The dream grew, tangling her with Dennis, giving her the sense of his hands on her, skimming over her body, lightly, tantalizingly. He touched her shoulder, then his hand slipped behind her neck and the clasp on her dress was undone.

Totally fascinated by the dream, she waited for what she knew came next. The material of her dress being pushed aside, then his touch on her skin. But instead of the analytical response she'd expected, she felt an explosion deep inside her. She gasped when his hand cupped her breast, teasing her nipple, and a rush of pure ecstasy ran through her.

It was too much, more than she could imagine, more than she could absorb, and time seemed to stop completely. Sensations bombarded her, and when his lips followed his hands, she cried out as she arched back.

This wasn't a dream. This couldn't be a dream. Nothing unreal could feel like this, and that's when she knew she was caught in human reality. His mouth drew on her nipple again, and she gasped, "Oh, no. No." Reality was everywhere, intermingled with needs and desires that were consuming her. "No."

She opened her eyes to see Dennis moving back,

his body partially over her, his shirt open and his hand on her stomach. Her bare stomach. Her dress was down to her waist, her breasts exposed, and her humanity raw and needful in a way that terrified her.

This wasn't a dream at all. She had no idea where the dream had stopped and reality had begun. No idea at all. Warring thoughts stunned her. Part of her, surely that humanity that had been forced on her, wanted to reach out for Dennis, to pull him back to her, to feel his hands on her body, to lose herself in him.

But the other part, the real part, knew how horrible this was. Despite the fact she had known a pleasure that had been almost pure fire, she jerked herself back from it. If her kiss with him had been foolish, this could only be categorized as a catastrophe, an earth-shattering mistake.

She moved back and away from Dennis, his touch completely gone from her now. Awkwardly pushing herself up against the cold brass of the headboard, she tried to tug her dress over her breasts. She was vaguely aware of Dennis receding, his features lost in the shadows of the room.

"Oh, no," she breathed in a choked voice, her hands shaking horribly as she tried to pull the black material up and refasten the clip at the nape of her neck. She gave up. There was no way she could do the clasp, so she held the material over her breasts and just tried to breathe again.

Dennis was very still, not saying a thing, but she could feel him watching her. "Why...why did you insist on doing this?" she muttered.

"I'd never push myself on you," he said in a tight, rough voice.

She could hardly blame him for that when she'd been the one reaching out to him, demanding more from him. "No, of course you didn't. It wasn't that. I meant, you insisted on bringing me home. I told you it wasn't a good idea, I knew it."

"We hardly thought it out," he said.

She tried to move back farther, but the headboard was ungiving against her spine. She hadn't thought out anything, but right then her one clear thought was this should have happened with Francine, not her.

This should have been different, the way it had been ordained, not with her going crazy with all the flaws of humanity centering in her.

Self anger burned in her now, pushing away the other fires that she had gotten a glimpse of moments ago. "Even humans wouldn't do this. I mean, we just met and suddenly…"

"You're right, absolutely right," Dennis said.

He stood, and she could feel her horror and fascination growing in equal measure when she saw the way his pants barely contained the evidence of how involved he'd been in their contact. But he didn't seem embarrassed by his body, or by what had happened. She heard him exhale roughly as he redid the buttons on his shirt. "We'll take it slowly."

She couldn't keep looking at him without those dammed human emotions tearing at her. If she'd been human, really human, she wondered, what would have happened? No, she didn't have to wonder. She'd seen enough of these encounters to know exactly what humans did when they wanted something this badly, when they wanted another person.

"No, we won't," she said, looking down at the rumpled bed. "This shouldn't have happened at all. It's wrong. Really wrong."

He was silent, and when she finally looked up, Dennis was closer, standing over her, the moonlight at his back all but hiding his expression. "Are you married?" he asked abruptly.

"No."

"Engaged?"

"No."

What could she say that would make him leave and let her deal with this mess and the ramifications that were soon to come?

"Are you involved with someone?" he asked.

The only human she seemed to be involved with right now was him, involved in trying not to ruin his destiny. And making a mess out of everything. Dennis, if he was anything, was an honorable man and she knew right then what she had to say to make him leave. "Yes, I'm involved."

He exhaled sharply. "Why didn't you say something?" he asked as he tucked his shirt in with sharp, angry jabs.

"You never asked."

He motioned toward her with one hand. "What about this?"

"It was a mistake and I'm so sorry," she whispered.

"For God's sake, don't apologize," he muttered and turned away from her. The next moment he was gone.

It was what she wanted, but that didn't stop her from experiencing an emotion that she identified right away. Sadness. Her eyes burned oddly and her lips felt unsteady. Sadness. A horrible, horrible human emotion. She flinched when the front door closed with a soft thud.

For a moment she knew another emotion, true regret. Then she pushed it aside. There should be no regret, only over what she'd allowed to happen. There should be no regret over Dennis being meant for Francine. She had no right to even think in those terms.

Yet when she tried to imagine Francine with him, it made her sadness deepen.

She heard a car start and then the noise of the motor gradually died out. When the last sound was gone, she sat there, staring into the darkness. Nothing made sense. Nothing.

"Welcome to the quirks of humanity," Miss Victoria said softly.

Angelina flinched at the sound of the voice, but this time it wasn't in her, it was real. Miss Victoria was there, visible, at least partially so, by the door with the moonlight filtering through her semisolid form making her look ethereal.

"Oh, Ma'am, let me explain," she said quickly, fumbling to fasten her dress. She never stopped talking. "Believe me, I thought I was dreaming, and the Council said to experience human emotions." She nervously smoothed the material over her breasts. But her touch only exposed a sensitivity in her nipples that caused havoc inside her at that moment.

"So sorry," she mumbled as she clutched her

hands in front of her, curling them into fists so tightly that her nails dug into her palms. "I...I'm so, so sorry. What a mistake. I thought I was doing the right thing, but I was wrong. I'm just so very sorry, that—"

Miss Victoria lifted one tiny hand and cut off her almost incoherent ramblings with, "It is enough that you realize how confusing human existence can be. We can only hope that no irrevocable harm has been done to anyone."

Angelina wasn't at all sure what harm had been done. She knew she didn't even dare to take stock of the damage right then. She wasn't at all sure she ever wanted to figure that all out. "Ma'am, he's gone. I told him—"

"That you were involved with another human?"

"Ma'am, I knowing lying is not acceptable, but I really thought it was a necessity at that moment. I really felt that he had to realize that this was a mistake and couldn't happen again. And it wasn't exactly a lie."

"Oh, we know your rationale for it. Quite intriguing. Though lies are not tolerated, Angelina, and you are aware of that, one does understand your motives."

"Thank you, Ma'am."

"And we believe that your own discomfort is enough of a warning in this matter."

Discomfort? An understatement. "Oh, yes, Ma'am."

"But, no more lies, either intended or implied."

"Absolutely."

Miss Victoria floated slowly across in front of the door and side windows. "Odd," she whispered.

"What is odd, Ma'am?" Angelina asked as she scooted to the edge of the bed and put her legs over the side.

"That human places tend to either change completely or be frozen in time." Her translucent hand stroked the delicate drapes that framed the doors and they stirred as if from the touch of a light breeze. "We never expected it to be this way still."

"You've been here before?"

"Once. A long time ago in human terms." Before she could ask why Miss Victoria had been here, the tiny woman began to shimmer as she grew more ethereal and moved a hand in Angelina's direction. "Take care, Angelina." She slowly dissolved and disappeared. *"And remember your directive from the Council,"* floated down from a distance.

"Yes, Ma'am," she said, then knew she was alone.

"Remember your directive." The words echoed in her and she brushed at her dress. But just that simple action brought back the images of moments ago with a clarity that was shocking. How did humans forget something like this? How did they get past foolish actions and go on with life? The answer was there before her hand stilled on her skirt. They didn't. She wouldn't. There was no forgetfulness for this sort of thing. She would just have to learn to deal with it.

DENNIS DROVE AWAY from the refurbished auto court with Angelina's words ringing in his ears. *"Yes, I'm involved,"* she'd said, shattering whatever illusions he'd allowed to form during the evening. *"This was a mistake."*

"A mistake," Dennis muttered into the shadows around him in the car as he drove down toward the beach. Dammit, he'd made mistakes himself, enough to fill a book, but Angelina had not felt like a mistake. He closed his hands tightly on the steering wheel, trying to kill that lingering feeling of her skin under his hands.

Instead of driving home to his beach house, he drove into the downtown area in the direction of his office. He only had a few hours before he had to be at work, so he decided to go to the office, sleep on his couch, then get going on the contracts Sam needed.

He slipped into the parking spot by the elevators and opened the door. But when the interior overhead light flashed, he knew that walking away from Angelina Moore was easier said than done. A purse, a shawl and a pair of shoes rested on the floor on the passenger side.

He reached over for the things, picked them up, and as he drew them toward himself, he caught that scent again. The damnedest thing. Meadows and sunshine and...something he could only call Angelina. It defied explanation, almost as much as his need for a woman who wasn't even available defied explanation. He regretted that he hadn't found out what sort of perfume she wore. Just so he knew what to avoid for now.

He sat back in the seat, fingering the soft wool of the shawl, and he closed his eyes. He'd never been a man to moon over a woman. Oh, he'd found a number of them fascinating. He'd had relationships, some more important than others. But none of them stood up to her smile, or the way it felt as if that expression could center his world or turn it on its ear.

And the way she felt when he touched her... Nothing in his past had prepared him for meeting Angelina, a woman he'd thought had stepped into his life right at the perfect time. Until he found out she was "involved" with someone else.

He almost hit his head when he realized how stupid he'd been. He'd been so stunned by everything, when she'd said she was involved, he thought of nothing but getting out of there. Involved? That wasn't married, or even engaged. That wasn't absolute or in anyway permanent, and she'd responded to him. God help him, but he could still feel the way her lips parted, the way her breast swelled under his touch. She responded totally and completely...at first.

He laid her things on the seat and got out of the car, then glanced at his watch. Four o'clock. He fought the urge to go right back to see her. No, he'd get a few hours sleep, then head back in the morning to find out just how "involved" she was with this man.

Chapter Eight

February 13th, 8:00 a.m.

Angelina woke to silence and the bedroom bathed in the cool light of dawn. She lay in the bed, the cool linen soft against her bare skin, and she stared at the ceiling. Sleep was good. No wonder humans spent a good third of their lives doing it.

She hadn't dreamed and without dreams, it was perfect. Nothing, where you didn't have to think or relive mistakes. And that was definitely a good state after her mistaking everything last night for a dream...at first.

She pushed herself up and swiped at her tangled hair to get it off her face. She'd never thought about the possibility of Miss Victoria having physical ties to this world. Especially not in a place like this.

She swung her legs over the side of the bed and stood, her feet pressed to the coolness of the hardwood floor. Actually, she didn't really know what this place was like. She had never seen the outside, and the interior had been dimly lit last night when she'd stripped off her clothes and climbed into bed.

She'd fallen asleep almost immediately, and hadn't known another thing until she woke now.

She looked around, then crossed to the armoire and opened it. Clothes hung there, casual clothes, sweaters, shirts, slacks and jeans. And a white terry cloth robe. She reached for the robe, slipped it on, then padded barefoot out the door and to the kitchen that opened to the living room over a long bar. A skylight overhead let in the pale light of the new day.

She opened the small refrigerator, looked at an array of food, but bypassed them all for a quart of milk. She'd barely turned with it in her hand when there was a loud knocking on the front door. She froze. Dennis was the only person she knew who knew about this place. She couldn't see him again. Never again. Even though some perverse part of her felt a twinge of pleasure at the thought of it. The sensible part knew it would be another disaster. She stood very still, hoping he'd just leave, but the knocking sounded again and again.

Finally, she spotted a round hole in the door. She put the milk carton on the counter and crossed to the door, where she cautiously pressed one eye to the hole. She hadn't known she'd been holding her breath, until she saw a stranger there and not Dennis, then she let go of her contained air in a rush.

She stood back and opened the door to the stranger. The man was fairly tall, she thought, with longer brown hair, a face she would have called rough with a full mustache and a deep tan. He wore a pair of bright red swimming trunks and had a towel draped around his neck.

"Welcome, neighbor," he said with a grin. "I'm

the welcoming committee, such as it is, and I'm here
to make you an offer you can't refuse." The grin
deepened. "How about a swim?"

She found herself smiling at him, partly out of
relief he wasn't Dennis, and partly because his enthusiasm was contagious. "Just who are you?" she
asked.

"The chairman of the welcoming committee."

"Do you have a name?"

"Paul Mason. I live right there." He flicked his
head to his right, and Angelina leaned forward to
glance outside. There was a circle of cottages, all
done in pale pink with light turquoise trim, and in
the middle was a swimming pool, fringed with palms
and carefully manicured gardens. The door on the
unit next to hers stood open. "And you're...?"

"Angelina."

"So, Angelina. How about it?"

"How about what?" she asked, trying to remember if she'd ever heard of a Paul Mason in her business.

"A swim? A dip? A plunge? Water aerobics?"

Swimming. She'd been swimming a few times,
very long ago, once in Greece, and once in Hawaii
just before the big eruption. A long time ago, now
that she thought about it. But it didn't appeal to her
right now. She had so many things to figure out.
"Thanks, but I'm not much of a swimmer."

"No problem. I'm a great teacher."

She bet he was, in any manner of things. The man
was charming in a human sense. "I don't think so."

"Oh, I get it." He pressed one hand to the doorjamb and leaned toward her, his voice getting a bit

lower. "I'll tell you something about myself. I'm not interested in anything but a swim." He shrugged. "Oh, not that you aren't tempting, lovely in fact, but I've sworn off women. Nothing but trouble."

She made a mental note to check out his romantic background and find out who screwed up so badly with him. "You sound pretty cynical."

"No, not cynical, just smarter." That grin was back again and totally endearing. Some woman would melt in its glow. He motioned into her place. "I forgot to get coffee yesterday, so I'm temporarily caffeine challenged. Do you have any in there?"

She didn't have a clue what she had besides the milk and the few groceries in the refrigerator. But she had seen a coffee machine on the counter. "I don't really know."

He stepped inside and looked around. "A carbon copy of my place, but with furniture. Did you rent it this way? No one told me that was an option."

"It came with it. Paul, I—"

"You don't have to fuss. I can make my own coffee." He started for the kitchen. "Aha," he said as he pointed to the coffeemaker, then picked up a ceramic jar right by it and opened the lid. "Double aha, coffee!" He checked out the machine. "Coffee, filter and water."

Moments later, he turned back to Angelina and spotted the milk on the counter. "Milk, too. Life is good, don't you think?" he asked as pulled off his towel, dropped it on the counter and grinned that grin at Angelina where she stood by the open door.

"So, how about that platonic swim to keep me company? I'm the sixth son in a family of boys, so

I'm not used to being alone or being quiet. I never even knew either state existed until I moved in here. I'm new, you're new. So, let's be new together? What do you say?''

While Paul was talking, Angelina heard a car outside and as she glanced over her shoulder, all the good feelings Paul had created immediately crashed around her ears. The black Bronco drove right up to the front of her place and into the parking slot. Dennis was back. Her ploy hadn't worked.

"Well, how about it?" Paul was saying, but her attention was on the man getting out of the car.

Gold wire-rimmed sunglasses hid the deep blue eyes, and the sunlight caught at the gold that streaked his blond hair. The gray silk shirt and tailored slacks were gone in favor of Levi's jeans, a well-worn leather jacket and a plain white T-shirt. The sight panicked her for a moment, and the only thing she knew was, he was back and she didn't want to be alone with him. Not here, not after what happened, or almost happened, last night.

"Angelina?" Paul said.

She looked at him. "What?"

"Cups? Mugs? Got anything to put the coffee in?"

"Oh, in the cupboard, I guess," she said.

Paul turned to the cupboards, and Angelina almost jumped out of her skin when Dennis said her name. "Angelina?"

She turned and he was right there, less than two feet from her. It was then that she noticed him holding something in his hands. Her purse. Her shawl and her shoes. "You left these in the car last night," he said.

"Oh. Thanks."

He stood there, his eyes hidden, and she hated sunglasses right then. She couldn't read his look at all and that only added to her nervousness, a nervousness that increased when he held her things out to her.

She took them carefully, not wanting any human contact with Dennis. He looked too appealing, too casual and too... She sought for the right word, but immediately rejected it when all she could come up with was *sexy*. She braced herself, certain the Council would surely intervene right then.

A bolt of lightning? A quick trip back to headquarters? She knew that anything they did was justifiable right then. She had no right thinking like that, or letting herself think that about any human male in those terms, especially this man. But there was no lightning, no zap that would leave her with a horrible headache. She understood.

They weren't doing anything because they were testing her to see if she had learned from her mistake last night. That was it. They were sitting back watching, waiting and they were going to let her sink or swim on her own.

She bit her lip, thinking hard about what to do, and wishing she could conjure up a physical barrier between the two of them. Then incredibly, there was an answer to her wish. "Angelina, coffee's ready."

Paul. The answer to everything right now. She'd all but forgotten about him, then there he was. Perfect. She hugged her belongings to her and saw Dennis look past her into the cottage. She could see she was on the right track when his mouth tightened. But she took no pleasure at all in the answer to her wish.

"Thanks," she said to Paul without turning to him, and almost dropped her things when she heard his voice right behind her.

"Good morning. Since I'm the official coffee maker around here, you're welcome to a cup. Can't vouch for the stuff itself, but it's hot."

Angelina saw the way Dennis looked from her in her robe, to a half-naked Paul, then back to her. For that slice of time, she almost thought she had some of her powers back. That she could read Dennis's mind, but that wasn't any more true than her thinking she'd controlled anything since this all began. Anyone could tell what the man was thinking about the situation, any human being with half a brain, and it made her feel sick.

"Oh, let me introduce myself. I'm Paul Mason, and you're...?"

"Leaving," Dennis said, then finally looked at Paul. "I need to get to work. Sorry for the interruption." The tightness in his expression caused a pain for Angelina somewhere behind her breastbone.

She couldn't do this. It was a lie, even if it was only by omission. "Dennis, I know what you're thinking, but—"

He shrugged that off. "It doesn't matter what I think. I can see you're involved."

"Paul's my neighbor."

"Convenient."

"Hey, buddy, hold on. Angelina was nice enough to take me in and—"

Dennis cut him off with an abrupt, "No explanations are needed. I just returned a few things." Angelina was startled when Dennis flicked the fringe of the shawl.

She pulled her belongings more tightly to her stomach and felt the heel of one shoe bite into her middle. But she didn't shift or change its position. The physical discomfort helped center her in some bizarre way. "I really appreciate your bringing them back."

He pushed his hands into the pockets of the leather jacket. "Have a good day." Then he turned and was climbing inside his Bronco before Angelina managed to take another breath.

"So," Paul said softly by her ear. "Don't tell me. You and the boyfriend had a fight last night. Now he's ticked off finding me here."

She flinched as Dennis closed his door sharply behind him and started the motor. "He's not a boyfriend, and we didn't have a fight."

"Isn't he the one who carried you in here last night?"

"How did you know that?" she asked as she turned from the sight of the black car disappearing down the street.

"I just happened to be up getting a drink of water, and I happened to see a guy carrying someone in here. Maybe ten minutes later he takes off, all but squealing his tires." He shrugged and spread his hands palms up. "Then this morning, the tension between the two of you is so thick I could cut it with a knife. What am I supposed to think?"

"You humans always read situations wrong," she muttered.

"We humans are into denial, aren't we?"

"What are you talking about?"

He turned and spoke as he walked back into the kitchen alcove. "Hold on. I make more sense after my caffeine fix." He reached for two big blue mugs he must have found in the cupboard and turned to Angelina. "Black or with milk?"

She swung the door shut, then crossed to the counter and slipped onto one of the stools at the bar. "Just milk. No coffee."

"Your wish is my command," he said.

When she finally looked up at him over the rim of her mug, he was studying her intently. "So, I can listen to other people's troubles forever. Want to talk?"

She almost wished she could tell him everything, that maybe if she said it all out loud, she'd see the logic in what was going on with her. But what could she say, that she was a fairy godmother who'd been forced to be human and was having a confusing time figuring out just how to respond to a human male who was intended for another human?

She took another drink of milk, then tried a partial truth, something he could understand as she lowered the mug to the countertop. "I am so confused by what's going on right now."

"With that guy?"

She nodded. "He's not right for me. And I can't get involved with any human...man. He's supposed to be with this very lovely woman who adores him.

I mean, she's his soul mate, but he's acting as if he'd like to be with me. But that's impossible.''

"Why's that impossible?"

"It's impossible on so many levels I can't even begin to explain it to you."

"He sees a beautiful woman and he likes what he sees, obviously."

She looked at Paul. "Do you mean that? Am I beautiful, I mean, as far as human beings go?"

He frowned at that. "Excuse me? Haven't you ever looked in a mirror in your life?"

She fingered the cold mug and stared into the milk in it. "Is that why he's doing this, because of how I look?"

"I'd guess that's a good guess on your part."

She actually relaxed just a bit. "Oh, if it's just looks, it's not going to last long, then, is it? Boy, that makes sense. What a relief."

If all Dennis was looking at was this human body of hers, there wouldn't be a terrible amount of damage. He'd get over it soon, and realize what really counted in love. Angelina drained the mug of milk and pushed it toward Paul. "More milk."

"Sure," he said, refilled the mug and scooted it back to her. "Are you in love with this guy, whatever his name is?"

"Me, in love?"

"There's no one standing behind you. You."

She recognized love in humans. She'd had a good eye for that, a special talent at spotting that soul-deep connection. But what she was feeling wasn't love. Love couldn't be a mixture of pain, joy, insanity, confusion and exhilaration that left a person exhausted, confused, and feeling worse than she'd ever felt before. No, that couldn't be what every human being was looking for, what humans cried for and some died for.

"His name is Dennis Benning, and—"

"Well, I'll be dammed," he said, cutting off her denial. "*The* Dennis Benning? The man who signs my paychecks?"

"Your paychecks?"

"I just started as the manager at Sanbourn Wineries. Benning money is involved over there, believe me." He grimaced. "Dammit, I wish I'd known that was the head honcho, I'd have insisted on him staying and having coffee."

The winery. Angelina remembered the place well from her assignment with Sam and Melanie. It had only been two months ago in human time, but it felt like aeons ago. "You're thinking of his father."

"The guy that was just here is the son? Man, Len Watson, the guy I'm replacing over at the winery, said he met the son a while back. Some strange doings about a mud slide and a break-in and the son of Benning being involved."

"That wasn't Dennis," she said quickly. Then amended that. "I mean, I don't think it was. It must have been the other son, Sam Harrison."

"Whatever," he murmured. "So, this guy today was Dennis Benning the second? Well, that doesn't surprise me, then. He comes over here, obviously ready to make up, then he sees me here, and he just backs off. I mean, he was mad as hell, but he just let it go. He's obviously like his old man. A down and dirty fighter in business, but a cold fish in his personal life.''

"Dennis might be a Benning, but he's not like his father at all. He's got his own law practice and he works hard and he's a warm, caring person. He just wasn't about to stay around here and...'' She was at a loss for a word there. "Well, you said it. He just thinks I'm attractive, and that's nothing to fight over. It'll go away very soon.''

"Wars have been started for beautiful women,'' he murmured, then took another sip of coffee.

"Stupid, foolish humans,'' she muttered.

"Condemning your whole species?''

"No, it's not my—''

She realized what she was going to say right when, thankfully, a shrill ringing cut off her words.

"So, are you answering it?'' Paul asked.

Angelina reached for the telephone on the bar. The plastic receiver felt very cold in her hand as she pressed it to her ear. "Yes?''

A strange woman's voice spoke to her. "Angelina?''

"Yes.''

"This is Marian from La Domaine.'' The waitress who had been so nice to her last night. "Mr. Summers wanted me to call and tell you he needs you in here at four this afternoon, and he wants you to wear something white, long and elegant, something that will go with his holiday decor for Valentine's Day.''

"Sure,'' she said, not even knowing if she had white, long and elegant in her limited wardrobe.

"And Angelina?''

"Yes?''

"He said your car is in the parking lot and you can't leave it there overnight again."

She'd forgotten all about it. She didn't even know what her car looked like, but she had to get it over here one way or another. Maybe she could have it towed today sometime. "I'll take care of it."

"Good, see you tonight." She hung up.

Angelina looked back at Paul. "That was my work. I've got a ton of things to do before I go back tonight."

Paul put his mug on the counter. "Okay. Work comes first. But let me tell you one more thing about us humans."

"Could I stop you?"

He shook his head, and said, "We rarely give up without a fight. Sometimes the fight's just postponed."

"What does that mean?"

"Benning'll be back."

"No, he won't."

Paul grinned. "Sweetheart, even with those sunglasses on, I could see the way he was looking at you. That guy's got it bad, and he's not going to give up."

She felt the flame in her skin and looked down into the empty mug. "He'll get over this physical thing quickly, then he'll be where he should be."

"Who are you to say where he should be and where he shouldn't be? You aren't calling the shots in his life."

He was right. She had no say in this at all. "I know that physical attraction isn't love. Besides, anything between the two of us is absolutely impossible.''

''Nothing is impossible in this world between two human beings.''

She looked up at Paul. ''I'm not the sort a human being like Dennis Benning could be or should be interested in.''

''Ah, I understand. You don't have the required social connections, do you?''

''Something like that,'' she said as she slipped off the stool, taking that simple explanation and using it. She had no connections in this world at all. Least of all with Dennis Benning.

Another human emotion clicked into place for her right then. Loneliness. And it hurt.

Chapter Nine

"Listen," Paul said, "I've got some things to do this morning and one of them is to go grocery shopping. Do you want anything?"

"Milk would be great, if you would. I'll get you some money—" Before she could stand, he cut her off.

"Pay me later. Anything else?"

She almost said, no, but stopped herself. "Hamburger buns, tomatoes, lettuce, pickles and mayonnaise."

"That it?"

"Unless you know where I can find a long, white, elegant dress."

"I haven't shopped for one of those for ages, but you could try the old town section, lots of nice, tony stores down there. Is it to impress the Bennings?"

"No, it's for work. I'm hostess at La Domaine."

"Work? Sure," he said with a wink. "I'll be back around noon with your groceries. See ya." With that he left.

Angelina poured the last of the milk into her mug. She took a sip and it was soothing. She needed something soothing as Paul's earlier words echoed in her. *"The guy's got it bad, and he's not going to give up."* She just hoped Paul was wrong about that, that Dennis was gone for good.

"Angelina, we are proud of the way you handled that situation." The voice was around her and inside her. *"You did not resort to manipulation or lies. Very well done, indeed."*

She didn't feel as if she handled anything well, least of all Dennis, and to have Miss Victoria congratulate her made her very uneasy. "Ma'am, he didn't let me explain."

"But, you told the truth. That is important. The man will figure things out in his own time. He will realize that Mr. Mason is just your neighbor, and a very pleasant human, we think."

"Very pleasant. Ma'am, is he in the system?"

"Yes, he is, although we seem to have hit a stumbling block in his pattern."

"He's pretty dogmatic about being through with romance. He's sworn off women."

"True, but we shall move on. He just needs to meet his soul mate, and when he does we shall see how strong his resolve is then. But, that is not your concern. Mr. Mason is being very well taken care of at the moment."

"Yes, Ma'am," she said.

"Now, go and mingle with humans. Be with them. Experience them. Your time is short."

"I don't have to be to work until this evening. But I do need to get a new dress."

"This is perfect. You can do what all humans do

when they wish to mingle and they need something special.''

"What's that, Ma'am?"

"Go shopping."

Shopping? That wasn't something Angelina had ever done or considered doing, not when she could have everything she needed with a simple nod of her head. "I guess I could do that."

"Good. Go and mingle." And she was gone.

Angelina glanced at the milk carton, then got up and went around into the kitchen area to open the refrigerator. She should have solid food, she supposed, but all she could find were bananas, peanut butter and a loaf of bread. She found a knife in a drawer and spread peanut butter on a bread slice. Bananas she knew about and liked, so she mashed one on the peanut butter, put another slice of bread on it and picked it up to head for the bedroom.

She needed to get dressed and go and mingle while she found that dress for work. As she stepped into the tiny bedroom, she had a fleeting memory of Dennis in here with her, and what had happened. Then the look on his face when he saw Paul here with her. This physical attraction thing had to go away, and she just hoped it went away quickly.

Her comfort was that physical attraction blazed furiously, but no fire that strong could last long before it burned itself out. No, Dennis would be concentrating on Francine soon, and if Mary was doing her job properly, that time would come very quickly.

"I'VE HAD IT. What is wrong with you today?"

Dennis looked up at his assistant, Audry, the first

person he'd hired when he'd set up his new office last year. Audry was middle-aged, heavyset, given to wearing blue, and was the most efficient assistant imaginable. She had a thing about green plants, putting them everywhere, and she was one of the most outspoken people he'd ever known.

He sat back in his chair and looked up at her. "Nothing's wrong with me. I'm perfectly fine, thank you."

"Do you want me to get Miss Clark on the phone for you?"

"Why? Did she call?"

"No, but from the way you've been acting, I'd say you've got lady trouble, and since you're heavily involved with Francine Clark, I figured you two must have had a fight of some sort."

Dennis sank back in his chair. She was right as usual, but had the wrong woman. "Audry, Francine and I didn't fight."

"Of course you didn't," she murmured.

"We didn't. Francine and I are just fine, thank you. Not that it's any of your business."

"If it affects your work here, it's my business. You pay me the big bucks to make you look good, despite yourself, I might add. Now, you sure you aren't frustrated…woman-wise?"

Dennis closed his eyes for a moment, but opened them right away when he conjured up images of Angelina in the short white robe, her hair in disarray, her eyes still touched by sleep, and Paul behind her. Making coffee, looking for all the world as if he'd— He cut off the thought of anyone spending the night. It was none of his business.

"Give me a break," he muttered.

"Well, if it's not woman trouble, it must be good old Mom and Dad again."

"No, it's not my parents, thank you. I just had a rough night." He nodded at the envelope she had tossed on his desk. "What's that?"

"Contracts. I just finished them. Your brother's all set."

He reached for the envelope, slid out the papers inside and glanced through them. "He'll want them right away. Get him on the phone for me."

"Are you sure you don't want me to get Francine on the phone? I thought she might need her shoe."

He was lost. "What are you talking about?"

She held up one finger, then hurried out of the office. In less than a minute she was back and holding out a simple black pump to him. "I found this on the carpet by the door. I just assumed that you and Francine..." She smiled slightly, a knowing smile. "Well, it's your office and it's empty at night and you've got that wonderful leather couch."

Her words bounced around him, taunting him, because of the miserable three hours he'd spent on that couch before going to Angelina's to spend another miserable time with her and Paul. But this didn't make sense. He took the shoe from her, but he could almost visualize the moment when he'd handed Angelina her things. Two shoes. In fact, one had been pressing into her middle and she hadn't tried to ease it. He could have sworn there were two shoes in her arms.

"Well, boss?" Audry asked.

He looked up at her. "What?"

"Francine. Do I call her or do you?"

"No, I'll take care of this. You could do a couple of things for me, though. Get the number for an Angelina Moore on Mockingbird Ridge. It's a new number, then wait about five minutes after you connect me to her, and get me Sam on the line."

For once she didn't ask any questions and Dennis was relieved when she left and closed the door behind her. He put the shoe on the desk, on top of the envelope with the contracts and stared at it. It was her shoe, all right. He must have dropped it. No, that didn't work. He never brought her things up here.

Something was crazy. Maybe it was him. After all, he'd become borderline obsessive about a woman he'd just met, yet a woman he could have sworn he'd known forever. *Crazy* barely began to explain his actions and feelings. The kiss, that moment in the bedroom, the need that made him ache, then finding Paul with her. The anger that tore at him. Yet a part of him was definitely still a Benning, the part of him that made him walk away without making an ugly scene.

His phone buzzed and he picked it up. "Yes?"

"Sorry, no listing for the lady."

The shoe was beginning to taunt him. "Okay, get me Lou Anders."

"The private investigator? Have we got trouble?" she asked.

"No, I just need information," he said. "And I don't need the third degree," he added and hung up.

He'd barely settled back in the chair when the buzzer sounded once more. He picked up the phone again. "Yes?"

"Sir, Mr. Anders is on two. Will that be all, sir?"

Her phony deference almost made him smile. "Thank you, Audry, just get Sam when I'm off from Anders," he replied, then hit the second line. "Lou?"

"Hey, kiddo, long time no hear. Last time you called it was to get the goods on that scummy accountant your client was being taken by. By the way, is the weasel in jail?"

"Three to five for embezzlement."

"Atta boy," Lou said. "Now, whaddya need this time?"

"Just a phone number." He gave Lou the information, then asked, "How soon can you have it?"

"Half an hour tops. Anything else you want me to do?"

Dennis almost said no, but something stopped him and he found himself saying, "Could you get me what you can on the woman, Angelina Moore? General background." If she wouldn't tell him about herself, at least he could find out something. "She's new to the area. Just don't leave any evidence about checking, okay?"

"Of course not. No one will even notice me."

Dennis grinned at that. The burly guy with jet-black hair and a face that showed every day of fifty hard years of living was far from what anyone would call inconspicuous. "Yeah, sure they won't."

"I'll be in touch, kiddo."

Dennis had barely hung up when the phone buzzed. "Yes?"

"Your brother on three."

He hit three. "Sam? The contract's done. It just needs your signature, then it's out of here."

"Great, I'd like to get it settled."

Dennis looked at the wall clock. Almost noon. "Why don't you come on over now, and we'll get it out of the way?"

"I've got a date with Mel for lunch. How about you join us?"

"I don't want to intrude on your time with Melanie."

"Tomorrow's the big Valentine's Day lunch, but today it's just a meal, and Francine's going to be there. Dos Gringos, the Mexican restaurant on Main. We've got reservations for twelve-fifteen. Meet us there?"

"Sure," Dennis said. He stood and reached for his leather jacket. He slipped it on, then went to grab the envelope. But the shoe was there. He hesitated, then picked up both of them and went out to find Audry.

The woman was at her desk surrounded by greenery.

"I'll be out for a while. If Lou calls, transfer him to my cell phone, and I'll be back around two."

"Are you going to look for Cinderella?"

"What?"

She nodded to the shoe in his hand. "Cinderella, the slipper? Remember your fairy tales when Prince Charming went looking for the woman whose lost her slipper?" She waved one hand at him. "Too fanciful for you, all that stuff about fairy tales and fairy godmothers, I'd guess?"

He glanced at the shoe in his hand. Fanciful? Fairy godmothers? Nonsense, yet why did it seem to ring a bell in him? He really was losing it. First forgetting he'd even brought the shoe up here, now thinking about Cinderella. "This isn't glass and I'm certainly not Prince Charming."

"You're the Benning prince."

"Give me a break," he said with a grimace. "No matter what my mother thinks, we are not royalty."

She laughed at that. "Well, don't ever tell her that. Okay?"

"I won't. I don't have a death wish," he said, finding a smile that he had been certain he didn't have any more. He lifted the shoe in her direction. "I'll get rid of this," he said, then left to meet Sam.

ANGELINA FOUND a couple of dresses in her closet, but nothing long, white and elegant. She dressed in a pair of jeans, put on a blue flannel shirt and a pair of nice suede boots, then grabbed her purse, called a taxi and headed out to shop.

Two hours later she was on the main street of Santa Barbara, just coming out of a shop where she'd found something long, white and elegant. A simple white crepe gown with a drop neckline, thin straps and a skirt that draped from just under her breasts. She only had fifty dollars left in her wallet after she'd paid, but the dress was perfect.

She stepped out of the store into a day beginning to gray with clouds and chill from a growing breeze coming in from the ocean. Her long hair curled wildly around her face, and with the large box with the dress under one arm, and her purse in her other hand, she stopped and looked around.

The street had been restored, with the building

fronts looking as if she'd stepped back over fifty years in human time. Ancient trees ruffled in the breeze, and the scent of brewing coffee was in the air. It was a lovely day, a human day, filled with things she'd seen before, but never fully experienced in her other form.

Miss Victoria had been right about mingling. She let people pass her by, smiling at them occasionally, and she looked in all the shop windows. She stopped at a little floral shop, then looked farther down the street. Not more than four doors down on the other side of the street, she saw something she recognized. The boutique Melanie had bought, The Place. The old bungalow had been redone, and made into a very upscale shop with jewelry and accessories, along with vintage clothing and designer household goods.

Angelina felt something in her that drew her to the shop, to see Melanie and be in a familiar place for a moment. It was akin to a longing that she didn't quite understand, but assumed was very human. But she knew what she was going to do. She stepped off the curb and started across to go to The Place.

DENNIS DROVE DOWN the street, the shoe on the seat laying on top of the envelope. Around the tenth time he looked at it, he decided he should have left it at the office, and left behind the visions of Angelina that seemed to come with its presence. It was taunting him, and it was making him crazy. When his cell phone rang, he reached for it and hit Send a bit harder than he needed to.

"Yes?"

"I got the phone number," Lou said.

"Great. What is it?"

He read it off to Dennis, then said, "I'm running into some trouble finding out about this Moore woman. Can't find a thing on her. No credit, no previous addresses, no police records, not even traffic tickets."

"Well, she's new to the area. Maybe she's from out of state."

"Maybe. There's an explanation, and I'll get the information. It isn't as if she just dropped out of the sky."

It almost felt that way to Dennis, but he said, "Get back to me." He ended the call, then entered Angelina's number. It rang twice, then a man's voice said, "Hello?"

"Oh, I've got the wrong number," he said, kicking himself for not writing it down when Lou told it to him.

"Who were you trying to call?"

"Angelina Moore."

"Oh, you got the right number. Can I take a message?"

Paul Mason. Dennis was shocked at the anger that rose in him at that revelation, and he said, "No thanks," and hit End sharply with his forefinger. At the same moment he was looking at the phone, he caught a flash of movement out of the corner of his eye, and when he looked up, he was horrified to see that someone had stepped off the curb and right out in front of his Bronco.

In a heartbeat, he jerked the wheel to the right, stood on the brakes, and as the odor of burning rubber, the piercing squeal of the tires on the road, and screams filled the air, he realized it was Angelina.

ANGELINA WAS LOOKING DOWN the street when she stepped off the curb and had just seen Francine coming out of the store when there was a sudden cacophony of sounds swallowing her up, and a tiny voice saying, *"Oh, gracious, no, Angelina, no!"*

She looked up, saw a car bearing down on her and she held out her hands in front of her, scattering her purse and the box with the dress, as if she could physically stop the vehicle from hitting her.

Dennis was there, it was him in the car, and time became a blur, a pummeling of sensations and sounds. Air rushed around her, a horrible roaring vibration, then sudden, awful silence. Dead, she thought, and the last person she saw was Dennis.

DENNIS FINALLY BROUGHT the Bronco to a shuddering stop after what seemed an eternity, but he had no idea what had happened. He just knew Angelina had been there, in front of him, and now there was a rushing group of people coming toward him and past him. He scrambled out of the car, jumped onto the ground and turned to look back.

Then he saw Angelina, with people surrounding her, but she was standing, hugging her arms around herself. He sprinted to her, and when he called out, "Angelina?" she turned.

For that moment in time, he knew a relief that went beyond joy. He slowed, getting closer. She was okay. She was standing. She was here. And he went to her, reaching out and the next moment he had her against him, holding her, his own trembling mingling with hers. "Thank, God," he breathed, his voice rough and unsteady. "I thought I hit you."

"Good Lord, Dennis, what happened?"

He heard Sam's voice, but he didn't let go of Angelina. He held on to her for dear life. Her arms were around his waist, and it seemed as if she were trying to become a part of him. He felt each shuddering breath she took, the way she exhaled, the softness of her against him. He could have killed her. He almost did, and he didn't understand why he hadn't. But he was eternally grateful she was here with him now and unhurt.

A hand gripped his shoulder. "Dennis?"

"It's okay," he whispered, opening his eyes and seeing Sam right by him. Sam, who usually was tanned, looked incredibly pale. "It's okay, Sam. It's okay."

Someone yelled to get a doctor, then there were sirens and Sam looked toward where Dennis had stopped his car. "Police," he said, then looked back at Dennis. "What happened?"

"I don't know. She walked right out in front of me. I thought I'd..." She shuddered in his arms, and he held her more tightly. "You're fine," he whispered to her. "You're fine."

"Anyone hurt?" someone asked.

Dennis kept his hold on Angelina, but he looked in the direction of the voice. A uniformed policeman was approaching, cutting through the crowd that was assembling. Then he saw Francine and Melanie approaching. "No, no one's hurt," Dennis managed to reply.

The cop stopped and looked at Dennis. "Oh, Mr. Benning, it's you. Are you sure you aren't hurt?"

It was like the restaurant last night, with Angelina on the floor, but everyone was more concerned about him. His anger wasn't at the cop, but at the mind-set of people who thought they had to cater to someone with money. "It wasn't me who could have been hurt," he said. "I was driving the car, I was talking on the cell phone, not paying attention, and I didn't see her until she was right in front of me."

The cop looked at Angelina who still had her face pressed into Dennis's chest. "She's all right, isn't she?"

She rubbed her face slightly against Dennis's leather jacket. "I'm okay," she whispered.

Dennis shifted back just a bit and moved his hands to frame her face as he tipped it up. Her blue eyes were overly bright with unshed tears, and he could see the way her chin trembled. "Are you sure, love?"

She stood very still, her hands at his waist, and he could see her try to form a word, but nothing came out.

"Angelina, tell me if you're hurt."

She closed her eyes, then shook her head. "No, no, I'm not hurt."

"Could be shock," the cop said. "She needs to go to the hospital and be checked out."

"No," she said quickly. "No hospital. I...I'll be fine. I'm fine."

She looked so distressed that it broke Dennis's heart. He softly stroked her cheeks with the pads of his thumbs. "That's not necessary. I'll take care of her," he said to the cop without looking away from Angelina. And he knew that's exactly what he wanted to do. He wanted to take care of her, and protect her and love her forever.

That last thought struck him to his soul, but he knew how true it was. Forever. He never wanted anything to happen to her and he never wanted her anywhere but with him.

"Come with me?" he asked her. She didn't move, didn't speak, and he did something he never did with any other woman before.

But he'd do it for her, because he knew that her answer would mean life and death. But not for her. For him. He begged her. "Please, come with me?"

Her tongue touched her trembling lips, then she said in a voice he could barely hear, "Yes, I'll go with you."

Chapter Ten

Angelina was alive. She was still human, and she
was thankful. She knew she should leave, that she
should be alone and get her thoughts settled and
composed. But mixed into that was a truth she had
only come to know since Dennis had kissed her last
night. She never wanted to let go of this human.
Never. He supported her. He was a rock. He was her
anchor. And that was terrifying for her.

Yet when she looked up at him, all she knew was
how precious he seemed right then. Human life was
precious, she knew that, but right then, this life was
more than precious. She felt her legs trembling, and
she kept her hold on Dennis.

He shifted and put his arm around her, pulling her
securely to his side. "I'll make sure she's okay,"
Dennis said.

"I can't believe that happened," she heard someone say, and glanced around Dennis to see Sam, with
Mel and Francine behind him. "I saw it and I still
can't believe it."

"You saw it?" Dennis asked his brother.

"I just came out of Mel's store and saw you coming down the street. I thought you'd misunderstood and were meeting me at Mel's, then you went right past and all hell broke loose. She was stepping right in front of you, then the car seemed to jerk to one side, literally swerve around her. It never touched her. Damned good driving." He clapped his brother on the back. "If you ever need a job stunt driving, just let me know."

"I don't even know how I did it," Dennis said, his grip on Angelina's shoulder perceptibly tighter now. "I'm just glad it worked." He started for his car, never letting go of her, for which she was relieved. If he had let go, she wasn't at all sure she could have walked two steps.

He got her to his car, pushed something onto the floor, then picked up an envelope before helping her into the passenger side. Angelina sank into the seat, thankful for the support, and saw Dennis hand Sam the envelope. "This is yours. Sign it, and messenger it or mail it."

"Sure, don't worry about it." He leaned around Dennis. "You be careful, won't you?"

She nodded. "Yes."

"Good. See you later," Sam said to Dennis, then Francine was there. She smiled at Angelina, a full, wonderful smile. "We're so thankful this all ended well." She held up the box from the boutique, a very crushed box with a distinctive mark on it. And a tire track right across the middle of it. "Your box didn't fare as well as you did, I'm afraid."

Dennis took the box, and turned, putting it in the car on Angelina's lap. He pulled back the crushed top, and remarkably, inside, the dress was untouched.

Long, elegant and still very white. "It looks okay," he said.

She nodded. "It survived."

Dennis looked at her and unexpectedly touched her cheek with the tip of his finger. "So did you," he breathed, then took the box and slipped it into the back seat before he turned to Francine.

"Her purse," Francine said, holding it out to him. "It's survived, too."

Dennis took it, then said, "I'll call you later."

"I'll be home by five." She leaned on tiptoes and kissed him on the chin, then patted his cheek. "You drive carefully, you hear?" she said, with no smile this time.

"That's the plan." He closed the door, and as he went around to get inside the car, she flashed a huge smile at him, and Angelina could read her lips. "Be careful."

Angelina turned to Dennis, saw him wave, then watch Francine for a long moment before starting the car again. Right then, Angelina recognized that she had discovered a new human emotion. She even had the name for it, as distasteful as it was to her. Jealousy. But how could that be? She knew for a fact that the Council had decreed Dennis and Francine a match.

She'd known that since the Council had tried to put Dennis and Melanie together. Miss Victoria had told her the Council had mistaken Dennis for his older brother Sam. Now Mary was on the job, working to give Dennis and Francine the opportunity to find each other.

Human emotions were horribly out of step with

logic. Dennis had almost killed her with his car, yet she was drawn to him more and more? To the point of being jealous of Francine? What interest could she have in Dennis beyond wanting him to find his soul mate? Interest?

She clutched her purse in her lap so tightly her hands were tingling from the pressure. No, it was concern for Dennis. After all, she'd seen him through a lot in the last two assignments. Concern. That was it. And she almost believed that until he unexpectedly reached out and covered her hands with one of his.

She froze, darting him a look, but he never glanced away from the road. "I'm so sorry," he said in a low voice. "I was talking on that dammed phone, and I never saw you until you were right there." His hold tightened on her. "I can't believe what happened."

She couldn't believe that all she wanted right then was to turn her hand over and hold on to him. To feel his fingers lace with hers—a simple action of holding his hand, of feeling connected to him. No, this went beyond concern. Way beyond, and she felt herself falling into human emotions so quickly she couldn't get her balance.

She tried moving away from his touch, but even when he drew back, she could still feel the sense of his hand on hers. Even when she looked out the window, she found herself having flashing memories of him kissing her. Biting her lip, she tried to clear her mind, but couldn't figure out how to banish the images. Not when the man was so close to her. Not when she only had to inhale to find his scent in the air.

"Are you sure you're all right?"

She was startled when Dennis spoke again, and she glanced at him. "I'm fine. I told you, I'm okay."

"You're shaking," he said.

She looked at her hands gripping the purse, and could see the unsteadiness. But tightening her grip didn't help. So, she let go and spread her hands on the leather. "That was horrible," she said in a voice that sounded tight and unnatural in her own ears.

"A nightmare." He shifted gears and she could see his hands were shaking a bit, too. He had been as afraid as she had been. She was just as human as any other human right then. Very human, she conceded, and that was why she had these urges to get closer to Dennis, to destroy the distance between them. Being human was a perverse condition, and that perversity surfaced in a rush when she saw Dennis's hand shake again.

Without a thought, she reached out and touched his hand with hers. Then her wish came true, as he turned his hand over and laced his fingers with hers. He simply held on to her, their hands entwined and resting on his thigh. Neither of them spoke as Dennis drove, and she admitted that the battle of trying to keep her distance from him was just too much for her right then. For that moment in human time, she simply let herself feel what every human being since the beginning of time had felt. And what she'd never felt before in her existence. Connected.

She knew it was wrong, but she couldn't force herself to pull free of the hold. She was inordinately aware of each breath he took, overlapping her own breathing. The way his hand felt warm and encompassing around hers. The way the engine sounded, and the slapping sound of windshield wipers on the windshield.

That startled her. It was raining, but she had never noticed it start. The windshield was rain streaked, and the sky outside ominously dark and heavy with clouds. It was then she realized they were out of the city, on a winding road that was high above the Pacific. Few cars were in sight, and the rain-slicked road climbed even higher.

"Where are we going?" she asked.

Dennis shot her a glance before looking back at the road. "Someplace to be quiet and calm down. It's not every day that something like this happens." He let her go then, to shift the gears, and she drew back to clasp her hands in her lap.

"Not every day," she echoed, clutching her hands tightly, and fighting a sense of loss now that the contact had been broken.

"It was like one of those awful dreams you have when you're a kid, where something's happening, something horrible, and you can see it all, but you can't stop it." He gripped the steering wheel and his grip was so tight that his knuckles whitened. "Did you ever have one like that?"

"I never dream," she said, but didn't explain that the only time she'd thought she was dreaming, she'd been awake and in bed with him.

"That's impossible. All human beings dream, several times a night, actually."

"Oh, you're an authority?"

"Just a human being who dreams." He looked at her again as he slowed the car. "I dream all the time," he murmured. "Sometimes the same dream over and over again."

Oddly, she felt that connection with him again, but this time he wasn't touching her. He'd just looked at her. Spoken to her. Talked about his dreams. She looked away from him, knowing she needed to do something to stop whatever was happening to her. "Where are we?"

"North of the city."

"That doesn't help," she said.

"Okay, we're here." He swung the car onto a narrow road with huge trees that blocked the rain and some of the light. Dennis maneuvered a sharp turn onto a short street that dead-ended into the bluffs.

Sheltered by ancient eucalyptus and sycamores was a house. It wasn't anything like the other beach house that Melanie and Sam lived in. This was older, more traditional, with gray clapboard siding, a massive stone chimney rising out of a steeply pitched, moss-covered shingled roof. It had a cobbled drive that led down to a three-car garage from massive iron gates.

Dennis turned off the road and onto the semicircular drive laid around a single towering pine tree. "Where is here?" she asked.

"My house."

"Oh, no," she said quickly. Not that. She didn't want to see where he lived, where he stayed away from the rest of the world. And she definitely didn't want to be in the house he would eventually share with Francine. "I don't think so. We'd better just go."

He stopped the car in front of the last garage door and turned to her, resting one elbow on the steering wheel. "No ulterior motives, believe me. You need to relax, and you need to take time to get over what almost happened. The ocean is remarkably therapeutic, and in the rain, it's almost hypnotic." He smiled at her, a smile that went right to her heart. "Besides, I have a vintage bottle of milk in my refrigerator. It would be a shame if no one enjoyed it when it was at its peak."

The smile was her undoing, and she looked away from it to the house. She was being foolish. It wouldn't hurt to go inside for a few minutes, to see what sort of life Dennis was making here, and to remember this place where he stayed on earth after she was gone.

She nodded. "Just for a few minutes. I have to be to work by four."

"Three hours. Plenty of time to unwind," he said as he pushed something on the dash that made the closest garage door raise. He drove into the garage and parked, then he got out, but before he could get around to open her door, she had climbed from the Bronco.

The chilly dampness of the air made her shiver as it touched her, and she hugged herself to cover the action. "You just moved in?" she asked, looking at boxes stacked in one section of the next garage area.

He led the way to some steps and opened the door at the top, then motioned her inside. "Been here three weeks. It took forever to find the place, but once I saw it, I knew this was it. It was built in the forties, and it's still standing. It's solid, and it's got the best view around.''

She stepped past him into a small room with laundry equipment on one side and cupboards on the other. Then she went through an open door into a huge kitchen with a vaulted ceiling. The room had wide plank flooring, off-white walls and ceramic counter tiles. It seemed to have every appliance that anyone could ever need. Cupboards were everywhere. A turret-shaped breakfast room overlooked the view through leaded-glass windows on three sides. A huge old-fashioned wooden table and chairs sat in the middle of it and plants lined the lower section of the wall.

"It must be wonderful to sit in there and just look out at the world."

"I haven't been home enough to do that yet, but I think you're right, it's got great possibilities," he said from behind her. Then he brushed past her and crossed to a huge refrigerator. He looked inside and came out with a huge jug of milk in his hand. "A very good year. How about a taste?"

"I'd like that," she said and moved over to the table. She pulled out one of the chairs and sat down facing the back windows. The ocean was starting to churn from the coming storm, and the rain drove waves into the surface.

Hypnotic. Yes, it felt like that. She rested her chin on her hands and stared at the failing light, and the vastness of the ocean to the dark horizon. "You really need to take the time to enjoy this view," she said.

Dennis was there, putting a large goblet of milk in front of her. "There are a lot of things I need to take time for," he murmured as he sat in the chair next to her.

"You seem to enjoy plants," she said.

"They're not mine. My assistant, the compulsive Audry, has to put plants in any bare space. I think it's against her principles to leave any part of a room bare." She looked toward him, and he lifted a glass he had in his hand partially full of amber liquid. "Brandy. I needed something a bit stronger than milk after that near miss. Do you want some in your milk?"

"Oh, no thank you." She lifted the goblet and tasted the milk. It slid down her throat, silky and rich. "Why would anyone ruin this taste with brandy?"

Dennis sat in the chair by her and fingered his glass on the table in front of him. "You don't drink?"

"I definitely drink milk," she said, lifting the goblet one more time.

"I mean alcohol. Since you don't eat meat, I thought maybe you didn't drink alcohol, and that's why you get so ecstatic about milk."

She smiled slightly at that, a bit surprised she could smile at all after what had happened. "I drink, a bit. I've had wonderful champagne." The Council had champagne that defied description. "And I've had brandy, Napoleon brandy." So long ago, during the war. "And once I tasted tequila, but that wasn't a great experience." That artist, the one who drew odd pictures that humans raved about, had favored tequila. So, she'd had a drink with him, and found it as terrible as his pictures. "And, of course, real nectar. A sensory pleasure."

"That's an odd way to put it, but I'd have to agree that some drinks are pleasurable to the senses."

"Milk certainly is. It's spectacular."

"I'll have to reevaluate milk some time when I have the inclination," he murmured, then motioned with his glass to the rest of the house. "Speaking of sensory pleasures, would you like to go in by the fireplace? There's nothing like a wood-burning fire on a rainy day."

"I've never tried that," she said and picked up her goblet.

"Never?"

"Oh, I've been to fires before, great bonfires, but just a little one in a fireplace? I've never really done that."

He looked at her oddly, then shrugged. "Well, now's the time to see what it's like."

He stood and she followed him through what was probably a formal dining room with a balcony off of it through glass doors, but with no table and chairs. Then into the living room.

The ceilings, crisscrossed with heavy beams, soared above hardwood floors and a massive stone fireplace in the middle of a bank of windows on the back wall. There were no furnishings in here, except for a wonderfully old-fashioned hooked rug with mellow cabbage roses woven into a pale blue-and-gray design. It was at least twelve feet square and centered in front of the hearth.

Dennis crossed to the fireplace, took stacked logs out of a niche in the stone facing and began to lay a fire. "As I said, I just moved in a few weeks ago, so excuse the lack of furniture. I just haven't had time to find what I want. My old furniture really didn't fit in here."

"Too small?" she asked as she went nearer to him, onto the rug.

"No, too modern, all black and white." He struck a match and touched it to the kindling under the logs. There was a snap and a crackle, and as the wood started to catch, he stood back, then slipped off his jacket. He laid it on the rug, then crouched in front of the fire again. "This place just isn't a black-and-white house."

"No, it isn't," she said as she sank down on the carpet and crossed her legs Indian-style facing Dennis and the fire and the rainy day through the windows.

He prodded at the fire with a poker, and she was fascinated by the way his T-shirt strained across his shoulders as he worked on the fire. "What do you think would fit here?" he asked as he put the poker down and turned toward her.

She fingered her goblet and looked around the space. Rain streaked the windows, and the fragrance of wood smoke touched the air. Despite the fact that the room was almost bare, it felt right. Too right. When Francine was here, she'd decorate it and love it, the way she'd love Dennis. Angelina took a drink of the milk, hoping it would take away a strange taste on her tongue.

She cradled the goblet in both her hands and looked past Dennis at the fire in the hearth. "I don't know. I'm sure you or...someone will figure it out."

Dennis came over to drop down by her side to face the fire. "Antiques," he said, then took a sip of his drink.

"What?" she asked, not daring to look at him when he was so close to her.

"Antiques. I think they might fit right in here. You know, large and dark and mellow. Comfortable pieces that have a history. None of this cold, plain, new stuff. Definitely no plastic or acrylic."

She chanced a glance at him, at the fire flickering across his features, setting soft shadows at his eyes and throat. The man was wonderful to look at. A human who looked good no matter what he did. She wasn't sure, but she thought that a human like Dennis had to be very rare indeed. Almost as rare as a fairy godmother who felt painfully human. "Definitely no plastic," she breathed.

He finished the last of his brandy, reached over to put his glass on the wooden floor by the carpet fringe and turned back to her. "Maybe lots of plants." He smiled slightly. "Although, I tend to be less than nurturing with anything that's green with leaves."

She looked away from him, the sight of his teasing and that slight smile too much for her to absorb when he was this close. So she looked at something that she knew, something that she could look at forever and not be confused or bothered. She looked out at the ocean. "It's beautiful, isn't it?" she whispered as she motioned with her goblet to the view.

He was silent for so long, she wasn't sure if he heard her or not, but when she looked at him, there was no smile, just hooded eyes watching her. "You're beautiful," he said softly.

She felt incredible heat in her face, and she turned from him to put her goblet on the floor. Physical attraction, lust, that's all this was. And she had to remember that. She had to remember Francine, and the edicts of the Council. She couldn't lose sight of that, she told herself, no matter how scrambled her thinking was becoming.

She should never have come here. She knew that clearly, but before she could do anything to leave, Dennis touched her on her arm. And she couldn't remember what she was supposed to remember. All she knew was the pressure of his fingers on her, that connection that riveted her to the spot. She tried to think of something to say, something that wouldn't sound insane right then. "We haven't even known each other twenty-four hours," she said.

But he didn't withdraw. She felt him shift closer, felt him move his hand up her arm to her shoulder. He was so near that she could hear each breath he took and she was fascinated by the sensations tumbling over her and through her. Human sensations, all-encompassing and completely disturbing.

"I've known you forever," he whispered, his lips by her ear, the heat of his breath brushing her, and she trembled. "And I've been waiting for you forever."

Chapter Eleven

Angelina turned slightly, shocked that he was saying things she was feeling. In a blur, his lips found hers, his heat breathed into her, and she moaned at the intensity of her reaction. How could pleasure bring such pain, and how could pain produce such pleasure? She opened her mouth to him, and moved closer, circling his neck with her arms, and relishing the taste of him on her tongue.

She'd watched millions of kisses over the ages, great kisses, kisses that changed the course of history, but she never suspected what a kiss really was. If she felt connected to Dennis before, she felt bonded to him now. She could sense a band circling them, sealing them together, and she went closer, wondering if it were possible for a human being to get lost in another. To stop existing and live in another human.

If she could have figured out how to do it, she would have melted into Dennis, to be part of him, to feel his heart beat in her, to sense every atom of his being. Her need for the man was overwhelming, frightening and thrilling all at the same time. Crazy, insane, she thought, yet when she and Dennis fell back on the rug together, she willingly tangled her legs with his. When he reached for the buttons on her shirt, she only regretted that he had to move back a bit from her to do it.

His hands pulled her shirt open, then his touch was on her bare stomach, his fingers branding her skin, searing her to her soul. The fine material of her bra was gone, and when he cupped her breast, she marveled at the raw ecstasy that filled her. She strained toward his touch, her breast swelling, and when his lips found her nipple, she was startled at the intensity of her reaction.

She arched even more, burying her fingers in his hair, pulling him even closer, and she cried out when he drew on her nipple. It tugged at an ache that was materializing deep inside her, an ache that throbbed to life, and she held tightly to him, terrified that he'd stop, that this would dissolve and be a dream.

But this time she couldn't blame it on a dream. She was wide awake and she wanted this human passionately. She wanted to be closer to him than was possible, to feel him against her, and to know what it was to be loved by Dennis Benning.

That stopped her in her tracks. The world froze and began to disintegrate the fire inside her. Love? She wanted to be loved by Dennis? No, no, she couldn't want that. She couldn't. But she knew that that was exactly what she wanted right then. She wanted to find human love, and she wanted to share that journey with Dennis.

The humanity that had been conferred on her to teach her a lesson had driven her to this insanity, and she didn't know how to stop it. Or if she wanted to stop it. And that was the most terrifying thing of all to her.

Dennis had told Angelina the truth, the absolute raw truth. He had known her forever, and he'd wanted her forever. That fact was there, defying logic, defying the reality that he'd met her less than twenty-four hours ago. When he kissed her, when he touched her, when he felt her respond to him with such abandon, he knew that he'd found the other part of himself. A part he hadn't even known he was missing until Angelina was there.

He tasted her, and touched her, and heard her moan softly. His tongue teased her nipple, felt it swell and harden, and his hand pressed to her stomach. He wanted her more than he'd ever wanted a woman in his life, and he didn't just want this. He wanted everything.

His fingers found the snap on her jeans, and tugged it apart, then he pressed his hand to skin, and slipped it lower, into the waistband. He felt her breathing catch, heard her soft whimpering, and his own body was beyond ready for her. He wanted his clothes off. Her clothes off. He wanted to be skin on skin with her, to feel every inch of her, to feel her want him as much as he wanted her.

"Dennis? Hello?"

The sound of his name being called startled him, and he prayed that he was hallucinating, but when Angelina jerked back, he knew the sound of his father calling out to him was very real.

"Dennis? Are you home?"

The voice was coming closer, and he knew that he

must have left the garage door open. For some reason his father had chosen now to make his initial visit to this house. He pushed back, the image of Angelina under him producing such raw need that he almost cried out from it. Her flaming hair was wild around her flushed face. Her lips were swollen from his kisses, and her breasts strained toward him, their pink nipples hard buds.

He would have given anything right then to have access to a wish, one simple wish, to have his father gone. To be alone with Angelina, just the two of them until he'd had his fill of her. But a part of him knew that he'd never have his fill of this woman. No matter how long they had together, not even an eternity.

Wishing wasn't an option right then. Reality had to be faced, and he forced himself to move back and ignore the uncomfortable tightness of his jeans. As he stood, he heard Angelina moving, then as he turned, she was standing and fumbling with the buttons on her shirt.

"My father," he whispered to her in a rough voice. "I'll get rid of him. Don't move." He hesitated, then went to her, cupped the back of her neck and kissed her quickly and fiercely. He made himself let her go and turn from her, one of the hardest things he'd ever done.

"I'm sorry," he said over his shoulder as he headed for the door to the dining room, thankful that his body was easing.

"I am, too," he heard her say as he went through the door and into the dining room.

"Dennis?" his father called as Dennis touched the door into the kitchen and pushed it open.

His father stood just feet from him in the kitchen, his gray topcoat slightly damp at the shoulders, and a fedora in his hands. He smiled at his son, but the expression seemed tight. "There you are."

"This is a surprise," he said as the door swung shut on the rest of the house.

"I had Martin drive me over so I could talk to you without your mother listening to every word I said." He laid his hat on the counter, then slowly undid his overcoat as he looked around the kitchen. "I like this," he said, almost to himself. "Very nice."

His father looked back at him, and for the first time, Dennis thought his father looked old. He glanced past Dennis at the counter area. "Do you have a drink?"

"Brandy?"

"Perfect."

He crossed and poured a glass for his father. "Do you want to sit?" he asked, motioning to the table in the breakfast area.

Dennis felt nervous and edgy, partly from the fact that all he wanted to do was go back to Angelina, and partly because he'd never seen his father like this before. He'd always been so controlled, so distant, but now he seemed almost vulnerable. Dennis took the chair by him, and turned to look at his father who sipped the brandy.

"Very good," he murmured, then set the glass on the table. "I wanted to tell you something. I guess there's just one way to do it, just say it."

Dennis stared at the older man. Was he sick? Was he dying? "What is it?" he asked a bit abruptly.

His father almost smiled. "Oh, don't worry. It's nothing bad. Nothing's wrong, not really. I've just been doing a great deal of thinking since I found Sam, and I've finally figured out that life is short, way too short to live it any other way than happily. I've missed that most of my life. You've been a joy to me, and now Sam, well, two sons. A man has to be blessed to have the two of you as sons."

"Father, I—"

"No, let me finish. I came to tell you to do whatever it takes for you to be happy. Don't settle for anything less in this life, but for real love and commitment. Don't consign yourself to prizing prosperity and success, because it doesn't mean a damned thing without having someone you love with you."

Dennis stared at his father. The man he thought wouldn't have known love even it hit him in the face, had fooled him completely. "You and mother, were you ever in love?"

"I don't know. I think we probably were, on some level, around the time you were born. But over the years…" His voice trailed off, then he finished the brandy and put the glass down with a slight thudding sound on the wooden tabletop. "That's over and done. No way to correct it or fix it or change it. What I'm worried about is you. I want you to know that I'll back you in any choices you make." He smiled slightly. "You know, I like the Clarks. I adore Melanie. She's wonderful for Sam, and Francine is a lovely girl. Very nice, indeed. I know that she's very important to you."

"Yes, she is. She's a terrific person. The Clarks turn out wonderful daughters, in my opinion."

"And you have good taste in women, my boy," his father said as he stood.

Dennis got up and faced him. "Do you mean what you said about backing me no matter whom I choose or what I choose to do?"

His father touched his shoulder. "Yes, I mean that." He exhaled. "Now, I need to go home and have a talk with your mother." He grimaced slightly. "I'm not looking forward to it, either. But it's something I must do."

Dennis felt the older man's tension, then his father did something Dennis could never remember him doing before. He hugged Dennis. For a brief moment he held tightly to him, then he stood back. His father nodded, crossed the rom to pick up his hat, then headed for the laundry room door.

Unexpectedly, the door to the dining room swung back and Angelina walked through into the kitchen. Her hair was tamed into a loose braid at her neck and she entered the room with a determined smile, saying, "Oh, yes, I think we can really do something with these rooms. Decorating is such a personal thing that one does want to make very sure it's done properly."

Dennis stared at her, heard her, but couldn't believe any of it. She was acting as if she were an interior decorator, talking nonstop and never looking at him. He started toward her, aware that his father had stopped at the exit and had turned to look at her. But before he could get to her, she was moving into the kitchen, waving her arms at the space. "Very,

very nice," she said, and looked at his father. "Don't you agree, sir? Your son has a lovely home here. Just incredible. One of a kind."

"Yes, I do agree."

She was right in front of his father now, her hand held out to him. "Angelina Moore, Mr. Benning. Lovely to meet you."

"My pleasure," his father murmured with an inclination of his silvered head as they shook hands.

"I was just talking about the house with your son, figuring out what it needs to make it a real home. He thinks antiques, and I have to concur. They would fit perfectly, if he can find the appropriate pieces for the period the house was built in. They would make it a pleasure to come home to, don't you think?"

"Yes, a pleasure," his father repeated with a smile. He obviously was enjoying her, and that made Dennis feel good, until Angelina turned to him.

"I have to get going. Back to work, you know. Now, I need to call for a taxi."

"No, you don't—"

"Oh, but I do." When she turned to look at him, the smile slipped and he saw something akin to sadness in her expression. He didn't understand any of this. "I have to get back to the city."

Then the smile was there, brilliant and breathtaking as she turned to his father. "Sir, you wouldn't by some stroke of good fortune be going anywhere near the main part of the city, would you?"

"I can take you," Dennis said quickly.

"I don't want you to go back out in this storm if your father is going my way."

"Of course, son, don't be foolish. I have the car

right outside, and it would be a pleasure to take this lady into the city.''

"Oh, that's wonderful, sir," she said. "I'm ready anytime you are.''

"I'm leaving now.''

"Perfect." She turned to look at Dennis. "I don't think we need to talk again. You're on the right track. Good luck," she said, then went out the door in front of his father. His father glanced back, smiled at him, then left.

Dennis stayed very still, feeling as if he'd been run over by a steamroller. And the memories were there again, a beach house, night, someone breezing in. No, they were here in front of the fire, Angelina in his arms. The dreams, they were there too, dreams of the woman.

He turned and pressed his hands flat on the countertop. He couldn't think straight. He had memories of things that never happened mingling with memories that happened just moments ago, tangled up with dreams. His body ached and he felt a level of frustration that tore at him.

"Angelina," he rasped. The woman was driving him crazy. Yet he knew he could love her.

He closed his eyes and let that thought sink into him. Love. He could love Angelina, a woman he'd known less than one day. But that was wrong. It wasn't a matter of could he love her. A part of him already loved her.

He grabbed a clean glass, poured a healthy shot of brandy into it, and drank it in one gulp. It burned a fiery path down his throat, but it did nothing to diminish how he felt. He put down the glass and hurried out into the garage.

The door was still open, and the rain had let up, but it was raw and damp and gray. He went to the Bronco, around to the passenger side and opened the door. The box and her purse were gone, but the shoe was still there, sitting on its side on the floor.

He picked it up and stared at it. Cinderella's slipper. And he knew where Angelina was going to be at midnight. The same place he'd be.

ANGELINA SWALLOWED hard as she settled into the soft leather seats in the back of the luxury car, the ruined box with her dress in it on the seat next to her, and her purse in her lap. Mr. Benning sat across from her, a man she knew well, but a man who didn't know her at all. He was in pain, she knew that much, and he'd given Dennis the green light to love Francine. She could love the man for that. He'd taken that burden from his son, but she had the feeling he'd assumed his own burden by doing that.

"I know that she's very important to you," his father had said. And she could still hear Dennis saying, *"Yes, she is."*

And she'd almost messed that up. She'd almost hurt something that would be precious to Dennis just because she'd acquired another human trait, selfishness. She wanted what she wanted, and for those few moments in Dennis's arms, she'd forgotten about anyone but the two of them.

"Where can I drop you?" the older man asked.

She could barely meet his gaze now, not when she

thought about what she and his son had almost done. "Just…just downtown."

"Anywhere in particular?"

She remembered a landmark during her shopping spree. "Yes, the theater, the one that's just been re-done for live performances."

"Oh, yes, they're having ballet there next week. It's a wonderful addition to the community." He reached for a phone set into the plush side panel near him, pressed a button and said, "Downtown, Martin, by the Victory Theater."

He slipped the phone back onto the cradle, then looked at her again. "So, you are an interior decorator?"

She couldn't lie, but she couldn't tell him the truth. So, she told a form of the truth. "I'm a facilitator, of sorts. I help people make connections that improve their lives and their happiness. I, hopefully, make their lives better—more fulfilling." She almost choked on the last sentence. She'd almost destroyed Dennis's life. There was nothing worse for a human than losing that window of opportunity to find that one person you were created to be with. "They have what they need and what they want."

"Do you grant wishes, too?" he asked, the shadow of a smile on his face. "No, that's what fairy godmothers do, isn't it?"

She knew her mouth dropped at his words. "What?"

"Facilitator is a corporate buzzword, not something from a fairy tale."

Fairy tales. Lies and dreams all mixed into one frothy story. "No, this isn't a fairy tale. I was just discussing Dennis's...Mr. Benning's decorating ideas. He loves that house, and I think he's wanting to decorate it for a family.''

"Very perceptive of you. I believe you're right. And there is this lovely woman he's seeing, one of nine children actually, so if they marry, which I find highly probable, I'm sure they will have children.''

Even he knew they should be together. "And you would be a grandfather. How does that sound to you?''

He chuckled at that. "I think I like that idea. Yes, very much indeed.''

"How about your wife?''

Surprisingly, that brought a real laugh from the man and for a flashing instant, she saw Dennis in him. The crinkle of the eyes, the way his mouth lifted, the shadow of his son in the father. "Oh, my, Emily would fight the label of *Grandmother,* I'm sure. But, she'd come around. She'll make everyone miserable for a time, but eventually...she comes around...when she's had time to think about things.''

She doubted Emily Benning would ever enjoy anything about Dennis and the Clarks, no more than she enjoyed Sam being in her life. But maybe she would have a "spell'' and figure out no one was noticing, then come around a bit. "You're probably right. How could anyone ignore a child?''

His face sobered, tingeing it with a certain grayness, and she knew exactly what her words had produced in the man. He'd had a son, Sam, and known he was his son, but virtually ignored him for most of his life. He was trying to make up for it, but having a wife who only saw Sam as a product of an impulsive affair was making it hard to have that son in his life. "Some can," he murmured as the phone in the side panel rang.

He hesitated, then reached for it. "Yes? Thank you, Martin." He put the phone back and looked at her. "We're here." He glanced out the window. "The theater."

As the car slowed and pulled to the curb, Angelina picked up the ruined box and her purse. "Thank you so much, sir."

"My pleasure," he said with a slight smile.

"I wish you well, you and your sons," she murmured, then the door was opened from the outside and she slipped out onto the wet sidewalk. The rain had let up, but the chill lingered in the air. She looked back inside the car and nodded to Mr. Benning, then the chauffeur closed the door.

In front of the theater a woman in bright red overalls was changing the announcement on the marquee above the ticket booth. Cinderella...A Fantasy for All Ages."

A perverse coincidence, Angelina thought and turned from the sight.

"Hey, where are you going?"

She looked behind her and saw Paul heading down the street toward her. He wore corduroy slacks, an open-necked white shirt and a tweed sport coat. A very pleasant man, she thought, but nothing like Dennis.

She stopped that thought and concentrated on forming a smile for him. It wasn't hard. She was glad to see a familiar face that didn't bring complications with it. "What a surprise. What are you doing down this way?"

"Just tying up some loose ends." He stopped in front of her. "By the way, your door was unlocked, so I put your groceries in your refrigerator."

She never thought of locking her door. Locks were foreign to her, but she knew they were essential to humans. "I forgot to lock the door, but thanks for getting that stuff for me and putting it away."

"No problem. And someone called. I think it was that Benning man, around noon."

No, that made too much horrible sense. Dennis was calling her and got Paul right before he almost hit her. Human coincidence was weird, but not that weird. She shifted the box to under one arm and fumbled in her purse to get her wallet. "How much do I owe you?"

"Forget it. It wasn't much, and I need a favor from you as payback."

She looked up at him. "Me? A favor?"

"Since you're a woman, and I'm not." He grinned at her. "I need to get a gift for my sister-in-law, and I don't know where to go. She likes weird little household things, things that don't do anything, but look good. Did you find any fantastic place that sells stuff like that while you were shopping?"

She almost told him she didn't know, but right then she looked up the street and saw The Place. Going up the steps at that moment was Francine's youngest sister. She couldn't remember her name, but she was over twenty, cute and a Clark. She hadn't heard about her being assigned to anyone, but Paul would be perfect for her.

"I found a store like that today, now that you ask, and it's great. Very unique gifts." She motioned down the street. "It's over there, in the old bungalow, The Place."

He glanced where she pointed, then looked back at her. "Perfect," he said with that grin, then gave her a mock salute and headed off down the street.

She watched until he was almost to The Place. A car pulled up on the street and someone got out. Francine. She got to the steps that led up to the entry just as Paul got there, and he stopped, said something to her, then stood back to allow her to go up the steps in front of him.

Angelina had a twinge of discomfort at the sight of Francine looking so carefree and happy. Then Paul followed her into the shop and the door closed. Angelina turned away from the sight and saw the woman who had been fixing the marquee at the theater. Now she was putting up a poster in a side window, a poster of Cinderella in rags facing her fairy godmother.

Fantasy, fairy tales, so far from the truth that it was almost laughable. But right then Angelina wouldn't have minded a magic wand and some magic words so she could make everything right for everyone. Especially Dennis.

She waved her hand to get a taxi and as the yellow car stopped in front of her and the door opened from inside, she thought of waving that wand, fixing everything. Then she could go back to where she belonged.

She'd failed the Council's test big time. It was just a matter of waiting for the score to be handed out.

Chapter Twelve

As the ornate clock in the reception lobby at La Domaine Restaurant struck midnight, Angelina realized that she was in trouble.

She'd come to work on time, in her long white dress, had worked all night. She'd blocked her thoughts, doing what she had to do, distracted by the constant flow of couples celebrating Valentine's Day early. And Miss Victoria wasn't there. She hadn't felt her presence for a while. For that she was very grateful. Especially when she thought about the afternoon.

Blocking those thoughts, she started to leave the lounge, but when she opened the door, the clock struck midnight, and she ran right into Dennis.

She'd slipped off her white heels and had them clutched with her purse to her middle, and she barely kept from dropping them when she saw Dennis in the doorway.

He was wearing the leather jacket again, but with dark slacks and a banded-collar blue shirt. Devastatingly handsome. The words came to her and she couldn't deny them. She conceded that, right along with admitting to a perverse pleasure that he was there, but it was all topped with an anger that he was making this so hard for her and for himself.

The human heart was an odd thing, experiencing good and bad emotions at the same time in equal measure. No wonder humans were confused all the time.

"Ah, here you are," he said, the shadow of a smile on his lips.

"Here you are, too. The question is why?"

"Well, I'm not here to ask you about decorating my home." He grinned at her. "Although, that performance of yours was priceless. I'm sure my father thinks you're an eccentric interior decorator, and he'd never guess what was going on just before he broke in on us."

"He thinks I'm a fairy godmother," she muttered, not measuring her words when her heart was beating so hard she almost felt as if she should hold it in her chest.

He laughed at that. "I doubt that he thinks that about you."

"Why?"

"Besides the fact they don't exist, if they did exist, everyone knows that they're all short, fat and old. You just don't qualify."

"*Well, I never,*" Miss Victoria huffed in Angelina's mind. That startled her. She'd been so engrossed in Dennis's appearance that she hadn't sensed the lady close by until the moment she spoke. "*Short, fat and old? We are not amused by this. Humans are so misinformed, it is ridiculous.*"

"Absolutely ridiculous," Angelina muttered.

"What? Why? You're certainly not fat, short and

old." He grinned at her, a brilliant expression full of endearing humanity. "Nope, you're no fairy godmother."

"You don't know much about fairy godmothers," she said.

"Oh, and you do?"

She looked him in the eye, the wrong thing to do right then. The truth came out of her without her even knowing it was going to be said. "I know more than anyone about fairy godmothers. In human terms, I'm an expert."

"Be careful, Angelina."

He laughed again. "Okay, I deserved that one. I suppose the tooth fairy is a second cousin of yours?"

"He doesn't exist. That's a fable, just like Cupid is a fable."

"Careful. Do not let this human make you say something that will do harm."

"There's no little fat man in diapers running around shooting arrows at humans," Angelina said and shrugged. "Although, some humans could use a good shot from time to time."

"Why do I have the idea I'd be a target if you had a bow and arrow in your hands right now?"

"Calm down, my dear. He's only human."

That was so right. So very right. "What are you doing here?"

He held up a single black shoe. A black pump, just like the pumps she had at home. "Yours. You forgot it in my car."

She frowned at the shoe in his hand. "I've got my shoes at home." She remembered putting them in the closet when she was looking for white shoes to match this dress. Side by side. Two of them. "That's not mine."

"It's not mine."

"Then it's your girlfriend's," she said.

He sobered at that, but the intensity in his eyes was every bit as disturbing as the smile had been moments ago. "Are we going to stand here and argue about the ownership of the shoe?"

"Absolutely not," she said. "It's not mine."

"Prove it."

"What?"

"All this talk about fairy godmothers, try on the slipper like Cinderella did." He held up the shoe. "It's not glass, but it's yours."

She stared at him. "Cinderella never had glass slippers. How could a human being dance in glass shoes? I mean, think about it. How ridiculous can humans be when they make up fairy tales?"

"Angelina, this is not wise to attack human beings, especially when you are dealing with one. When you are one.*"*

"Better they wear leather from a dead cow?"

"That's disgusting," she muttered. "At least I have some sense." She was amazed at how much Dennis could infuriate her with simple words, or a simple look.

"And you're against fairy tales."

"I'm against the ridiculous. How realistic is a woman stuffing her kids into a giant shoe?"

Dennis stared at her, then the laughter came, a sound that surrounded her and soothed her and drew her to the man so strongly that she literally braced herself to keep from leaning toward him. "You've got me there,'' he said as the laughter trailed into a soft chuckle. "But reality isn't what fairy tales are all about, is it? Not any more than reality is what life is about all the time."

Her reality as she knew it was standing on its ear and never felt solid or sure. Surely human beings didn't go through their whole existence with this uncertainty and confusion. She could barely stand it any longer. And she couldn't stand being this close to Dennis.

"If that's all you need, I have things to do."

She would have gone around him to make her escape then, but he stopped her by blocking the doorway and not moving to let her pass. "That's not all I need." She chanced a look up at him, trying not to retreat from the intensity in his blue eyes. "I need an explanation. I need to understand what happened this afternoon."

"There isn't an explanation," she said quickly, hoping against hope that Miss Victoria would let it all pass and not bring her punishment down on her now. Right now she had no desire to worry about the Council. There were no words from her superior inside her, and she breathed a sigh of partial relief, then said, "Now, I have to go."

When he didn't move, she tried to go past him into the hallway, but she ended up having to push between him and the wall. She tensed as the action made her feel far too much of his body against hers before she was free to head down the hallway and away from him.

But there was no escape. He was right there by her, falling into step beside her, talking as they walked into the reception area. "There's always an explanation," he said. "Nothing just happens in this life without a reason. Cause and effect, you know? I know the cause, I know the effect, all too well, but I don't know why."

"Humans. You have to have an explanation for everything, don't you?" she muttered as she neared the desk where Summers was working over the reservation book. "Can't you just let it go?"

"No, I'm the kind of person who needs explanations," Dennis said doggedly.

"Remember that humans desperately need to make sense out of a life that really is very nonsensical."

Now, Miss Victoria chose to interject her wisdom. Making sense out of what happened was an impossibility for her. So how could she give him any explanation that made sense. "Too bad," she said tightly.

"Too bad?" Dennis asked.

Summers looked up, frowned with annoyance for Angelina disturbing him, then he saw Dennis and the smile came. "Oh, Mr. Benning, how lovely to see you." He all but fawned over the man. "Our dining room is closing, but for you, we will definitely make an exception. Just let me go and—"

"Thanks, but I'm not staying."

Again, there was a flash of a frown on the man's face, then it was gone as if it had never been, replaced by that ingratiating smile. "Of course, sir. As you wish." Summers flashed Angelina a look that made her feel vaguely like a bug he'd like to squash, then his full attention was back on Dennis. "I hope the replacement shirt was to your liking."

"Excuse me?"

"We sent a new shirt to your office. I was assured it would be delivered this afternoon."

Angelina had to call a taxi, but she didn't want to do it in front of Dennis. She knew he'd offer to drive her and she didn't want to be that alone with him as long as she was human. So, while he talked to Mr. Summers, she eased back, intending to go down the hallway to the phones by the rest rooms and then slip out the back way.

"I've been at the office since late this afternoon, and didn't see it. But my assistant might have signed for it. She was gone by the time I went back to work."

"That must be it. It's probably waiting there for you right now. A lovely shirt, identical to the one Miss Moore ruined last night. We hope it will make up for some of the inconvenience you suffered."

She was close to the hallway now, just a few more feet, and her instinct was to run like mad, but she was afraid of making any fast moves that would draw Dennis's attention.

"I didn't suffer anything, and I'm sure the shirt will be just fine," Dennis was saying.

She never took her eyes off Dennis by the desk, but right when she was about to turn and go to the phone, she felt a cold rush of air as the entry doors opened. Then someone called her name.

"Angelina?"

Dennis turned, Mr. Summers looked up at her, and she turned to the voice. Paul. She'd heard the human expression, *A sight for sore eyes,* and right then she understood it. Seeing him was such a relief. He was her buffer, the person who could get her out of here and away from Dennis.

"Paul? What a great surprise," she said, hurrying over to where he stood by the front doors. It seemed right to hug him, and she didn't fight the urge. He was fresh and cool from the outside air, and so very welcome. Then she realized that she was leaning on him, almost afraid to let go of him. She forced herself to move back and smile up at him. "What are you doing here?"

He looked at her with a considering expression. "Being very glad I got restless and went for a drive and saw this place. I remembered you said you were working until midnight and you didn't have a car, so I thought you might need a ride home."

She wouldn't have to worry about Dennis asking her to go with him. It all worked out and she was very grateful, until she sensed Dennis coming toward them.

"Mason?" he said.

Paul glanced at Dennis who came up by Angelina's left side.

"Benning, good to see you again."

"I'm taking Angelina home," Dennis said flatly.

"You never asked me," she protested.

He looked at her intently, then came even closer, speaking as if Paul wasn't even there. "I told you, I need an explanation. I'd like one tonight. I thought we could drive and talk and figure out some answers."

"No." She bit out the word more abruptly than she intended to, all the while wishing she could turn and run. But there was no way she could do that.

She couldn't make a scene here, not with Summers staring at her, and Paul caught in the middle of it. "There aren't any answers," she said tightly.

"You're wrong." He was so close his breath brushed her skin, and she shivered slightly. "Very wrong."

"No. I'm tired, and I just want to go home." That was absolutely true. "I'm going with Paul."

"Is that it?" Dennis asked, his voice low and tight.

"Yes," she whispered.

Dennis leaned toward her, and the next thing she knew, he cupped his hand at the back of her neck and drew her to him. The kiss came out of nowhere, with the intensity of a lightning strike. The contact was overwhelming, quick and hard, searing into her, jolting every emotion she'd wanted dead and gone, to new, devastating life.

Then it was over, Dennis let her go, and before she could take a breath, he was gone with the parting words, "Forget that, if you can."

She closed her eyes tightly, felt the emptiness without him, and one overwhelming truth stung her soul. She loved him. She really loved him.

She felt Paul touch her on the arm, then he was speaking softly to her. "Whew, sorry about that."

"So am I," she managed to whisper, then realized that she'd dropped her purse and shoes. She hunkered down, retrieving them with a shaking hand, stepped into her shoes, then looked at Paul. "Take me home?"

"Miss Moore?" Summers called to her from the desk.

Angelina glanced at the manager. "Yes?"

"Your car. Please, take care of it. It is not to be left in the parking lot overnight again."

"Yes, sir," she murmured, the car the least of her human worries at that moment. She turned and went to the entry and out into the chill of the night. Paul was right behind her as she stopped at the curb.

"What about your car?" Paul asked.

"I...it's not driveable," she said.

"You're in luck," he said. "Which car is yours?"

She stared at him. She'd never figured that out. And the other key on the chain didn't have a logo on it or anything. She searched in her purse for the keys, then drew them out. Paul took them from her, looked at the medallion attached to the ring and said, "Ah, a Volkswagen. No problem. I've been working on them most of my life. Used to have a Bug when I was younger, and that thing ran on spit, baling wire and bit of gas now and then." He looked past her and pointed to a white VW parked near the side of the lot by a brick wall.

"Just let me take a look and chances are, I can get it going for you." He started toward it and she hurried after him.

"Oh, no, don't bother," she said quickly as he got to the car and went around to the front. "Just drive me home and I'll take care of it."

"It's no bother. Besides, I owe you big time."

She almost missed what he said, she was so bothered trying to figure out what she'd do when the car started and he handed the key back to her. "You're going to get dirty," she said, anything to get him to stop.

He disappeared under the hood, and as she inched

closer, she could hear him humming softly. Then he
looked back at her over the open hood. "It looks
good to me."

He held the key out to her. "Give it a try."

She stared at the key. She knew where it went, but
after that it was nothing. "I'm telling you, you don't
have to do this. They...they have..." Who were
those people? "Yes, mechanics who do this."

"And I told you I owed you. Let me do something
for you."

"You don't owe me. You bought my milk and
things for me. I owe you."

He came around to her. "Listen, you told me
about that shop in old town, The Place. I went there,
found the perfect gift and met someone. Oh, I'm not
talking romance, here. I'm talking a bright woman,
pretty, funny, someone I could be very good friends
with."

"Good friends make the best lovers," she replied
without thinking.

"No, not lovers," he said firmly. "Friendship is
all I'm interested in."

"I'm sure that Edward VIII said that about Mrs.
Simpson."

"What?"

"You remember, the future king of England in the
thirties gave up his throne to marry the woman he
loved, a commoner...a divorced commoner. In truth,
he saw her as a friend first, a gentle confidante. He
certainly wasn't looking for a romance that would
make it impossible for him to be king."

"You're either a history buff, or you were eaves-
dropping on the two of them."

She bit her lip hard, and tried to laugh. "I was hovering over them when he told her he was so happy to have a real friend, that he just wanted someone he could really talk to and be himself with. And I was there when his brother George found out Edward was going to abdicate so he could marry the woman he loved."

"Oh, sure, and that'd make you over seventy years old." He grinned at her. "I have to say, you look damned good for someone of your advanced years."

A faint noise got his attention, and he slipped a beeper out of his pocket. "What in the—?"

"Trouble?"

"It's the security page from the winery. Some problem." He pushed the pager back into his pocket. "I need to get over there." He opened the driver's door and slipped inside. A moment later, the little car chugged to life. Leaving it running, he got back out. "Bingo. I told you, they're just temperamental."

"Thanks," she said, staring at the little car putting and shaking, but definitely going.

"I need to get out of here. Will you be okay now?"

"Oh, sure, fine, just fine," she said.

"Good." He flicked her chin with his fingertip. "Drive carefully."

She nodded as he strode across to a large white pickup truck. "Paul?" she called as he opened the door. "This woman you met, are you going to see her again?"

"You bet I am."

"That's good."

He pulled the cab door open and the light from

inside spilled out onto him. "You bet it is. Francine Clark will be one terrific friend," he said, then got in and closed the door.

Angelina stared at him as the truck started, then backed up and drove out of the lot and into the night. "Oh, no," she moaned as she leaned back against the side of the idling car. Francine? That couldn't be. Not Francine. He was suppose to meet the other Clark sister. He had to have the name wrong. If he meant it, she'd not only messed up her time down here, but she had caused more trouble for Dennis and Francine.

Angelina closed her eyes and murmured to Miss Victoria.

"I'm so sorry. I've made such a mess of this human thing."

There was no answer from Miss Victoria, and Angelina concentrated. But there was no sense of her. "Ma'am?"

Nothing. That meant one of two things, both the Council and Miss Victoria were deliberately staying quiet so she could hang herself with more rope. Or Miss Victoria was with the Council deciding her fate right now. If she had to choose, it would be the rope scenario. That or banishment or clerical work or even being an assistant for Mary. She deserved anything they threw at her.

"Stupid, stupid, stupid," she muttered.

"Are you still practicing for the job?"

She didn't have to open her eyes to know her night had just gone from extremely bad to terrible. Dennis. He was there again, and when she took a sharp breath, she could catch a hint of the scent that clung to him. This wasn't fair, not fair at all. She never even had a chance to collect herself and figure out what to do before things happened again and again and again.

She knew that a nod of her head or a simple motion of her hand wouldn't whisk her away from here. Humans didn't have the luxury of taking themselves out of life, and she certainly didn't have that luxury now. She braced herself and opened her eyes, and right then the clouds in the sky parted and the moon was bright.

"No," she breathed, any other words impossible with Dennis so painfully near at that moment. Dennis. Not just another human, but Dennis. Unique, and compelling and so horribly easy for her to love...if she could. She stood very still by the idling car and just wished for it to be over quickly. Then she'd figure out what to do next, how to survive five more days of humanity.

Chapter Thirteen

Dennis had driven all the way down to the ocean before he knew he couldn't go home. He couldn't enter the house where Angelina had been with him and survive right now. Not until he made sense of what happened. At the Coast Highway, he turned around and headed to the closest bar that he knew about...in La Domaine.

He'd been certain Mason and Angelina would be gone by now, that he could go inside, sit in a dark corner and be left alone, once he got rid of Summers. But he was as wrong about that as he'd been kissing Angelina one last time. The kiss had only burned the need for her deeper into his soul.

He'd seen her tense at the sound of his voice. Her whispered "No" played havoc with every nerve in his body.

He could see the old Volkswagen was idling, but there was no one else in sight. "Where's Mason?"

"He got paged and had to leave. What are you doing here?"

"I came back for a drink. The bar's still open and

I could use something bracing right about now. I thought you would be long gone.''

"I'm leaving," she said, but didn't make any indication she was going to get into the car.

"Your car's working, I see?"

"Paul got it going."

She stood very still not more than two feet from him, and he knew she wanted him to leave. But he couldn't just walk away again. He'd finished with that. If she wanted out of this, she'd have to do the walking this time.

"Well?" he finally said when she started to fidget with her purse.

"Well, what?"

"Go ahead." He motioned to her car with his head. "Get in the car, drive it away from here and go home. That's what you want to do, isn't it?"

She looked away from him and muttered, "Of course, it is. Just go and get your drink."

"I'd rather stay here. I'm worried about you, about lingering problems from the accident this afternoon."

"Why? Your car never touched me."

"Shock does strange things to human beings. It can take a passionate woman and turn her into an interior decorator. Now, in my opinion, that's damned serious."

She didn't smile at all, but just stared up at him, then finally said, "I'm fine."

"I'm not," he said, the truth coming from nowhere, but he didn't apologize for it.

She turned from him as if he hadn't said anything, then slipped into the small car and closed the door with a resounding thud. Through the glass he could make her out as she gripped the steering wheel with both hands, then moved and hit the turn signal. She jumped as if the flashing light startled her, then she turned the signal off.

He saw her take another deep, hard breath, then grip the gearshift and jerk it downward. The gears ground horribly, and she let go of the shift as if she'd been burned. She'd said she was a terrible driver, but he had no idea how bad she was until then. She grabbed the gearshift again, ground the gears, pushed and shoved the stick up and down. He flinched. When the car motor finally died, he thought it probably had done so in self-defense.

She sank back in the seat, and even then, she was endearing to him. Dammit, she touched him on so many levels he couldn't begin to understand the strength of his reactions. When she moved to touch the key in the ignition, he rapped on the window and she jumped sharply before looking out at him.

Even in the moonlight, he could see her cheeks were flushed and her mouth set in a stubborn line. He made the motion for her to roll down her window, and when the glass barrier slid out of the way, he said, "Clutch. Maybe you won't drop your transmission."

She looked at him as if he'd lost his mind. "Clutch what transmission? Why?"

"So you can shift gears." He looked at the total confusion in her face. "This *is* your car, isn't it?"

"Someone left it here for me," she said.

"You don't know how to drive a standard, do you?"

"A car is a car," she muttered. "I've seen standard cars a million times."

"But you've never driven one, have you?"

She bit her lip, then flashed him a frown. "Humans drive cars," she muttered. "I am a human. I can drive a car."

"Not this car."

She exhaled on a hiss, then opened the door so abruptly she almost knocked him backward when it swung out at him. He moved back, then she was out, standing by the car, with her arms crossed on her breasts. "Okay, why not? I can turn it on, and I can pull the stick to shift it. You tell me why this car is so different from the others."

He would have laughed out loud if she hadn't been so deadly serious. "Let's make this simple. With a standard transmission, you have to shift through every gear and use a clutch with your foot to make the shift possible. If you don't use your clutch, you can't shift, and if you can't shift, your car won't go forward or backward. It's that simple."

"Simple? That's simple?"

"It is if you're used to it."

"So, you're saying unless I clutch and shift and things, this car is useless?"

"To you, it is."

"Oh, great, terrific." She threw her hands up in the air. "Okay, I'm a reasonably intelligent human being, and I can make this work with the clutch and the shift."

"The car won't survive, and whoever left it for you, isn't going to be happy if you trash it."

"They are already unhappy," she muttered.

"Can I make a small suggestion?"

She looked at him, those eyes wide in the moonlight. And he pushed his hands deep into the pockets of his slacks. The urge to reach out and touch her was overwhelming. "I need a taxi," she said abruptly.

"No, you don't, you need a ride. And I'm here."

"I'll take a taxi," she said with a sharp shake of her head. "I can call from inside."

"Dammit, this is déjà vu, isn't it? You stranded and me with a car, and you denying that you need a ride. It feels as if this is the sum total of our existence...or at least a punctuation mark between other fights."

"I'm not fighting."

"Good, because Summers is going to be a bit annoyed if we have a knock-down-drag-out in his parking lot, and in the end, that car is still sitting here."

"You can drive that car somewhere and leave it, so he won't see it here in the morning," she said, reaching back inside the car and taking out her purse.

"I could drop it off a cliff."

She turned back to him, the moonlight bathing her face in soft light. A frown tugged at her feathery eyebrows as she said, "I've messed up everything, so it doesn't matter if you want to blow the car up."

"How about a sensible tow to your house?"

Before she could say anything, rain fell, and not gentle rain. A deluge that came from the heavens and blotted out any light. He moved toward Angelina and slipped off his jacket to drape it around her shoulders. "Come on. Let's get out of this."

She clutched the jacket at her breast and didn't

fight his suggestion. He took the chance of reaching out to catch her by her upper arm through the rapidly drenching leather. "Come on."

He felt her stiffen at the contact, but she ran with him through the storm to his car. After he got her inside, he hurried around and got in behind the wheel, then slammed the door on the storm.

"Oh, no," she said as she wiggled to get out of the wet leather.

"Don't worry about the jacket—"

"The keys. They're still in the car." She pushed the jacket onto the floor by her feet. "Someone could steal it."

"You didn't care what happened to it a few minutes ago," he reminded her as he ran his hands over his wet hair. "Besides, the mechanic's going to need the keys to tow it." He picked up his cell phone and called the towing service and while he relayed the information, he watched her slip off her shoes and drop them on the floor.

"I didn't know it was going to rain," she said with a sigh.

"Fairy godmothers don't forecast the weather, do they?"

She swiped at her hair, tucking it behind her ears. And she suddenly looked incredibly young and vulnerable. "We...they aren't weather people, or psychics, you know."

He wanted to brush at the stray curls clinging to her cheek, but gripped the steering wheel instead. "No, I didn't know. Don't they do abracadabra and make things happen, like rainstorms?"

She turned to him. "No, they wouldn't do that."

Wind shook the car as rain drummed down on the roof. "Storms can hurt humans, and the protection of humans is a prime directive."

"What are you talking about?"

"Just thinking how dangerous storms are."

"This one solved our argument and neither one of us had to give in."

She sank back in the leather seat as rain battered the car. "This isn't solved. I'm not going anywhere with you. I'll just wait in here for the storm to let up, or…" She looked at his cell phone on the console. "I can call a cab from your phone."

"You could try, but you'll never get a cab up here at this time of night in this storm. They'll be snowed under."

"Then I can just sit here, and when the rain's done, I'll try to drive that car."

"You'll kill it and yourself. I can't allow that. I'll take you home." He started the Bronco. "That's settled."

"Hold on. Just hold on. This is not acceptable. I'm not going anywhere with you."

"Why do you always have to do this, fight me tooth and nail when I'm just trying to help?"

Angelina grew very quiet, and he didn't know what he expected, but it wasn't to look at her and see her leaning against the door on her side. Her eyes were closed and her wet hair clung to her face and temples.

"Angelina?"

She didn't move.

"Okay, forget it. I'm not going to force you to do this. I'm tired of it. All I want is to make sure you're safe, to do you a favor...." He exhaled. "Okay, I admit to an ulterior motive. I thought during the drive, we'd be able to talk uninterrupted. There, that's the truth. Now you tell me why you don't want to go with me. And don't use Mason as an excuse. That guy treats you like a brother."

She turned slowly and looked at him. "Just take me home, and don't come inside."

"That's it?"

"That's it. If you can't do that, I'll get out and take care of myself."

As he headed down to the road, the windshield wipers barely kept the windshield clear enough to see, and he drove slowly.

Neither one spoke until they were almost to the highway, and Dennis turned to look at Angelina. She sat very still, one hand resting on her heart, then other balled into a fist on her lap. He could see the tension in her jaw and neck, and right then he made a decision.

When he'd promised to take her home he fully intended to do that, but he altered that promise when he knew that if he took her home and left, that was it. Whatever had been happening between them would be over. It had been luck she'd been there when he went back, that Mason was gone and she couldn't drive that car. Maybe Fate was handing him an opportunity on a golden platter. He was going to take it.

Instead of turning south, he swung north and drove away from the city where the traffic thinned. At first he didn't think Angelina noticed, then he sensed her move, and when he glanced to his right, he saw her straining to see out the rain-streaked windshield.

"Just a minute," she said as he drove through the downpour. "The ocean's suppose to be on the right side. It was the last time you drove me home. This time it's not."

"Very perceptive," he said as he turned his wipers a notch higher to try to keep some visibility through the windshield.

She was looking at him now, he could feel it, but he didn't look at her. "What are you doing?" she demanded.

"Driving you home." He went a bit faster as the rain started to let up. "That's what I promised to do. And I won't go inside with you."

"But you're going the wrong way."

"It's not wrong, it's just different." He slowed the windshield wipers as the rain eased even more.

"Semantics," she muttered.

"It'll just take a bit longer to get there."

"Listen, I want to go home."

"I'm taking you home, I told you that. Just not *right* home."

"Now."

"In a bit."

"Right now," she said with more force.

"Can't you just sit back, enjoy the ride and let me talk?"

"No," she said. "I knew you agreed to that too easily. Now I'm a captive audience."

"More or less," he admitted in a low voice.

She sank back with an exasperated sigh. "You

know, this is kidnapping. That's a very serious thing to do.''

"Don't be ridiculous.'' He turned off the highway onto a side road that led up into the hills. "The rain's stopping, and it won't be dangerous. I just want to talk. Hear me out?''

"Do I have a choice?''

He pulled off onto the side of the winding road in a lookout clearing. He stopped the Bronco, turned off the motor and ignored the view of the city and ocean below through the rainy night. He turned to her in the shadows. "If you think there's nothing between us, just say so and I'll take you directly to your place and get out of your life.''

She pressed her back against the door and looked at him through the night in the car. Her expression was blurred, but he could hear each breath she took. He stared at her, an ache in him so very real that he grimaced. He wanted her. Not just on a physical level, but he wanted everything about her. He had a need in him for this woman that was staggering, yet he couldn't find the words to explain that to her.

"Well?'' he asked.

She waved a hand weakly, as if the action could ward off his words. But she kept silent.

He turned from the sight of her and gripped the steering wheel with both hands to stare straight ahead at the view of the night. The rain had suddenly stopped. "I just wanted to say that—''

"Maybe you shouldn't say anything,'' she interrupted. "I mean, maybe there are some things better not said. If you say things, sometimes that makes them more real than they really are. Do you know what I mean?"

He cast her a slanting look. "They couldn't be more real than they already are," he said.

"Dennis, no, you don't understand things." She moved closer, shifting to press a hand to the console that separated them. "You're confused and you aren't thinking straight."

"I'm thinking straight for the first time in my life." He needed contact and he touched her hand on the console. It felt like the only heat in his world at that moment, and he craved that heat.

She jerked back from him. "No, you aren't. Humans think that all the time, but it's not true. They don't understand things at all."

"Angelina?" he said, reaching out to make that contact again, but she moved quickly before he could touch her.

"No," she said, reaching down by her feet, and he realized she was putting on her shoes. The next thing he knew, she had her door open and was stepping onto the graveled clearing.

Dennis got out and circled the car on the uneven ground and went after Angelina as she walked awkwardly toward the road. He caught up with her just as she reached the pavement. "Angelina, wait."

She stopped, but didn't turn.

"You can't run away from this, Angelina. I won't let you. I've done that enough myself, and it doesn't help. It doesn't solve anything."

She turned slowly, and as the clouds began to filter away, the moonlight was there again. The same moonlight that had made her look so lovely earlier.

But now it showed something that looked like fear in her eyes. "Dennis, don't. I...I don't want to hear anything."

"Just one thing."

She pressed her hands to her ears, like a small child would to block hearing something that they were afraid of hearing. He felt his heart lurch, then he reached out and touched her hands, gently easing them down. "You have to hear this."

"Dennis, please."

He let her hands go and gently cupped her chin. "What are you so afraid of? Me?"

"Oh, no, not you, never you," she whispered in a shaky voice. "Never. I just don't want you to make a horrible mistake that could hurt everyone."

He looked down at her. Nothing about Angelina was a mistake, nothing. He'd made mistakes before, but this was right. It was so right. He moved even closer and whispered, "Angelina, I need you. I've needed you forever."

He felt her chin tremble, but she didn't move away from him. In the cool dampness of the night, she stayed there, and he realized she was crying. A single tear slipped down her cheek, glinting in the pale moonlight. "No, you don't," she whispered.

Dennis didn't need her, but Angelina knew then that she needed him. And the pain that admission produced in her made moisture fall from her burning eyes. Tears. She was crying, something she'd never been able to do before. Or something she'd never needed to do before. But right then, she cried and her humanity was a painful, horrible thing. All because of this man and her feelings for him. Love wasn't the good, wonderful feeling she'd always believed it to be. It hurt. It hurt so badly she could barely breathe.

"Oh, babe, don't be afraid," he whispered, his voice as shaky as she felt right then, and the kiss was as natural as if she'd been with him for aeons. His mouth found hers, hers responded, then she was in his arms. The cold of the world was shut out, and all that mattered was Dennis.

He searched her mouth with his tongue, his hands pressing her so close to his body that she felt as if she were fused to him. And the kiss seemed to draw at her soul. She could feel a part of her going to him, lost to herself forever. It was shattering, encompassing and terrifying all at the same time.

If Dennis hadn't been holding her, she didn't even think she could stand. A pervasive weakness was filtering through her, mingling with a fire that ran in her veins. It was beyond human emotions, beyond human need; it ran into a place that had no definition. A place she never knew existed before that moment.

Then everything shifted, shook and quivered, and for a moment she thought of an old human saying, something about a kiss making the earth move. And it was moving, shaking and rolling, and when she felt Dennis gasp, she realized the earth really *was* moving.

"Earthquake," Dennis breathed, holding her tightly to him. "Stand still. Stay right here."

She didn't argue. She held her breath and stayed right where she was...in Dennis's arms. And even though the whole physical world undulated under her feet, she felt secure and anchored.

"Angelina, I love you," Dennis breathed against her hair as things began to settle. "I love you."

If covering her ears would have stopped the words, she would have covered them. But nothing could take back those three words. And nothing could stop the repercussions she knew were coming. She pressed her hands to Dennis's chest, felt his heart hammering against her palms, then pushed herself away from him.

She stepped back into cold water, felt it swirling around her ankles, then with a rushing sound, the world gave way beneath her. In a flash, she was plunging down with water and mud, in a river of debris, screaming, flailing wildly for a handhold on anything to stop her.

Her one thought was that the Council had finally acted.

Chapter Fourteen

It seemed an eternity of falling and tumbling before Angelina landed with a splash in cold, waist-deep water. She was sitting in a shallow ditch, and before she could figure out if she was hurt or not, Dennis crashed into her, rolled into the water, then surfaced right beside her.

He shoved against the yielding mud, slipping twice before he got to his knees and faced her. She was gasping for air, water running down her face, her dress tangled around her and one strap broken. Dennis shook his head sharply, spraying water everywhere, then swiped his hair back from his face with both hands. "Are you all right?" he gasped.

She didn't know. But there wasn't any pain beyond a sensation pretty much like the one she experienced when she fell on the floor at La Domaine. "I...I think so," she finally managed to answer. "Are you?"

"In one piece," he said, pushing closer to her, as if seeing for himself that she wasn't hurt.

In the moonlight that broke through the cloud-scattered sky, she could tell that the Dennis she'd always known was hidden under plastered hair, mud and debris. His T-shirt was ripped at one shoulder and clinging to him like a second skin. He looked up the bluff that was backdropped by the cold night sky. "A giant water slide," he muttered, then he turned to her. "Let's get out of this ditch."

He scrambled to get to his feet, slipped once, then found his support and managed to stand. He held out a hand to her, a repeat of his offer at La Domaine the night before. "I have to say this, being with you is never dull."

Angelina took his hand, loving the feeling of his support and accepting it without an argument. When she surged up out of the cold water with his help, they both stood knee-deep in the water, their feet sunk in mire on the bottom, then Dennis let her go. But the contact came again, his hand gently cupping her chin as he peered at her intently through the night.

"What I wouldn't give for a flashlight," he muttered. "It looks like you got a scrape on her cheek."

"It's nothing." She moved her head back. "I'll survive."

He looked at her, then suddenly laughed, a sound that echoed up and down the vast ravine. She had no idea what was funny, none at all. They'd just fallen down a hill. One look up and she could see it was more than thirty feet down the sloping grade. The Council was seriously upset. Beyond upset. First they'd sent rain to discourage Dennis, then an earthquake to warn her, but she hadn't been able to stop Dennis uttering those words, and now this.

"What's so funny?" she finally asked, feeling her feet sinking deeper in the muck.

He coughed slightly and his laughter drifted off. "Surviving. That's what you said about your dress earlier." He touched her shoulder in a vain effort to try to pull the strap up. But it had broken in two. "It didn't survive this."

"I'm not going to survive this ditch if we don't get out soon," she stated and tried to move to the edge, but her feet got stuck and she almost tumbled back into the water. She would have if Dennis hadn't grabbed her hand.

"Steady," he said, then pulled her with him toward the edge of the ditch.

He let go of her to lift himself up and out of the water, then he hunkered down and reached for Angelina. She grabbed his hand, and as he literally pulled her up into the air, she realized that her shoes were gone. They were lost somewhere in the mud and water. She was up by Dennis, above the running water, and she dropped to the mushy ground to catch her breath.

"You are not hurt, are you, my dear?"

As Dennis hunkered down by her, she looked up at the cloud-filled sky and muttered, "This wasn't my fault."

"Of course it wasn't," Dennis agreed. "It was the rain and the earthquake. Although, if you'd stayed in the car..."

She glared at him. "You're the one who kidnapped me, and I tried to make you stop. Didn't I?"

"You tried," Dennis replied as he grimaced, looking at his muddied, soaked clothes, back at her, then up at the bluff. "Well, this is a fine mess."

Angelina stared at the long, white, elegant dress that had been reduced to a muddied rag that clung to her. "All that money," she moaned. "It's ruined."

"I'd say that's the least of your worries," Dennis drawled. "We have to get out of here. It looks as if the ravine runs up that way." He motioned into the night. "It goes higher and it figures, it'll be drier. We'll go until we find a shallow part of the bluff and climb out."

"Doesn't anyone live around here?" she asked.

"Not a light in sight. And we're in the middle of nowhere."

"If we have to climb out, we have to climb out," Angelina muttered and scrambled to her feet.

"No shoes," he said, looking down at her bare feet. "That poses a problem."

"Don't even think of telling me to wait here while you go for help."

"I didn't plan to." Dennis looked her up and down, then actually smiled. The man was enjoying this far too much for her tastes. "The ground's pretty soft here, and if we hit a rough spot, I can carry you. God knows, I've done that before."

She glared at him. "You won't have to. I can walk. Just lead the way, and I'll follow you."

"Okay."

He started off across the oozing ground, and she noticed that he'd kept both of his shoes. Then she noticed the way the wet clothes clung to him, the slacks hugging his lean hips and the T-shirt, as dirty as it was, exposing the rippling motion of his muscles as he reached for support from the brush that grew out of the side of the bluff.

Stop it, she told herself, forget it, and forget everything he said on top of the bluff. As she awkwardly followed him through the night, she made herself a promise. Once they were out of this, she was going to ask Miss Victoria to let her go back. She knew she was in big time trouble as it was, so there was no point in prolonging this agony.

They went higher, made their way around a section of the bluff that stuck out farther than the others into the ravine. Without warning, Dennis stopped dead in his tracks. She barely kept herself from hitting him in the back.

"I don't believe it," he breathed.

Dennis felt Angelina grab at his shirt to steady herself, but he never looked away from the sight in front of him. There had been darkness ahead of him, shadows and night, then they rounded the outcropping and suddenly there was the looming shape of a house in the distance. It sat in the middle of a huge meadowlike clearing shadowed by giant trees, a towering Victorian with spires and turrets and light in a couple of windows.

He could feel Angelina's heat at his back when she asked, "You don't believe what? That we're in a soggy ravine in the middle of the night without any sign of so-called civilization?"

"Wrong," he said. "Take a look at civilization."

When she eased around him to get a look, he heard her gasp softly. "We're saved! I can't believe it."

He couldn't believe it either. And he couldn't believe the way she almost jumped up and down with relief. He looked down at her by his side, and also wondered how she could act as if nothing out of the ordinary had happened *before* their fall down the bluff.

He'd said something to her that he'd never said—never even thought of saying—to any other woman in his life, and she was acting as if he'd never uttered the words. She grabbed his arm and looked up at him, and the sight of her so close was achingly sweet. "Maybe they'll take us back to your car, or we can use the telephone to call for help."

"Sure, we're saved," he said.

She stepped out ahead of him and without a backward glance, she went out into the grassy clearing and headed for the house in the distance.

He watched her for a moment without following her, just letting the sight of her in the moonlight linger in him for a bit longer. He knew he'd meant what he said. It was crazy, after only knowing her for a day, but he knew he loved her as surely and as completely as he knew anything in this world. He loved her. But that didn't stop the sinking feeling in his stomach.

She was stubborn as all get-out and afraid of something, and whatever it was, it was making a wall between them and he wasn't sure he could get through or over. But he was going to try like hell to figure out how.

He followed her toward the house where soft light fell out of the tall uncurtained windows and moonlight caught on the moisture clinging to the wood-shingle roof. "This is so wonderful," she called over her shoulder as he followed her onto a brick pathway that led to a wraparound porch.

He didn't catch up with her until she was climbing the sweeping stairs. He followed her up onto the porch and stood beside her as she knocked on a dark, heavily carved entry door with an oval frosted glass inset in it.

She knocked again, then a carriage lamp on the wall by the door flashed on, catching her in its glow. He'd been right about the abrasion, an ugly mar on her face, but it was the dress that really caught his attention. It was still wet and clung to every curve of her body, to the swell of her hips, the length of her legs... Then she turned to him.

The wet fabric left nothing to the imagination, her breasts high and taut, her nipples pressing against the clinging material. His whole body responded, and he had to stay very still, concentrating on relaxing before she could tell just how affected he was becoming. "Someone's home," she said, her smile of relief painful for him.

"It looks that way."

The front door opened a crack and an elderly lady looked out cautiously. "Who's there?" she asked as light spilled out onto the porch through the slender opening.

"We need your help," Angelina said.

Pale blue eyes behind rimless glasses widened as they took in the sight of Dennis and Angelina. "Oh, my gracious sakes," she gasped. "Oh, you poor things." She opened the door all the way, and Dennis could see the dove gray dress she wore and the halo of silvery hair set in curls around her cherubic face.

One hand was pressed to her ample bosom. "What happened?"

"We were driving and it started to rain, then it stopped and we were out of the car when the earthquake struck and we fell down a bluff into this ditch, and..." Angelina stopped for breath. "We need to get a ride back to his car or to use a telephone to get help."

"Oh, my dears," the elderly woman said, looking distressed as she stepped back a bit. "Please, do come in. It is so cold out there."

Dennis hadn't noticed the cold until she'd said that, then he saw Angelina shiver. "Yes, thanks," he said and reached to touch Angelina in the small of her back to urge her inside. But he didn't make contact. She moved quickly into the house.

As he stepped inside past the little lady, she looked up at him. "Sir? Are you sure you are okay?"

He wasn't, but it wasn't anything he'd tell her about. He nodded, and as he stepped into the house, he realized that the carvings on the door were intricately formed variations of Cupid and angels. In the wide entry hall, he was hit by more forms of Cupid, from the border at the top of the ten-foot walls, to the intricately fashioned newel posts, to the balcony railing on either side.

Then he turned to Angelina who was by a massive arch that led into an old-fashioned parlor. She had twigs and leaves in her hair, mud streaking her face, a scratch on her cheek, and her dress was almost brown from mud with the one strap hanging loosely from the fabric. Her bare feet fidgeted on the polished floor and she looked up and down at the ceiling with murals set in wood-framed squares, then at the cupids supporting the rails on the bannister.

He saw the flash of a grimace, but it was gone when she turned to the old lady who had just closed the door. With Angelina's opinion of Cupid, this house had to border on subtle—or not so subtle— torture for her.

"Ma'am, where's your phone?"

"In the parlor," she said, motioning to a wide doorway on the right. "But, it went out an hour ago. The storm and earthquake must have affected it."

"Do you have a car we could use?"

"No. So sorry," she said with a sincerely distressed look. Then her face cleared. "But the good news is, there is room at the inn."

"Excuse me?"

"The inn." She motioned with her tiny hands in a circle around the foyer. "Why, here. The Victorian Inn. There is one room left, which is amazing when one thinks about it being Valentine's Day tomorrow. We are usually booked up for a year for Valentine's Day. If you would like to, you are very welcome to stay in that room, have a hot bath, then in the morning, phone service should be restored." She smiled at them. "Yes, yes, that is a perfect solution."

"Can't we walk back to the road?" Angelina asked.

"Oh, no, my dear. That would be impossible at this time of night. Much too dangerous." She shook her head, making the tiny gray curls dance merrily. "Far too dangerous. You both must stay until the morning comes."

Dennis looked at Angelina and saw that fear there

again. It broke his heart, but he didn't know what to do. She glanced at him, but as soon as they made eye contact, she looked away and spoke quickly. "Ma'am, what about the other guests? Maybe one of them has a car we could borrow?"

"Oh, my dear, it is well past midnight. One would not disturb one's guests at this hour. No, they are here to celebrate Valentine's Day. A very special time for them. We would not dream of interrupting their stay. So sorry."

"Yes, of course," she breathed, swiping at the skirt of her ruined dress. "I can see that wouldn't do."

"Then you will stay?"

Angelina shifted from foot to foot, then spread her hands a bit hopelessly. "I guess there isn't any other way, is there?"

"None," the tiny woman said firmly. "This way." She bustled over to the staircase, touched the head of one of the Cupid posts, then went up the sweeping staircase.

Dennis looked at Angelina, but she didn't look at him. She moved quickly after the lady up the stairs, and he went behind, taking the steps two at a time. At the landing they went to the right, down a short hallway with doors on either side with gold Cupid silhouettes with room numbers on them in red. They stopped at one marked 2, and the lady opened the door, then motioned them inside.

Dennis stepped into a small room that looked like part of an attic with a sloped roof, two dormer windows with window seats strewn with red pillows and the only real piece of furniture, a huge bed. It had massive posts, with carved cherubs in them, and a headboard carved to look like draperies being held back by Cupid on both sides. The spread was white satin, and rose petals were scattered everywhere.

An old-fashioned potbellied stove was tucked in one corner and he could see the glow from the coals inside and feel the radiating warmth.

"The bath is in there," she said, pointing to a closed door with another gold cherub on it. "A common bath is down the hall, the last door. There are plenty of towels and lovely, lovelies in both rooms."

Lovely, lovelies? He just nodded.

"And of course, if you wish, we could bring up some hot tea. You both look chilled. Surely after such a scare and having to walk so far, you could use some libation to warm you up? We could bring a dash of brandy, if you wish?"

Libation? Had this lady been a resident in the nineteenth century or something? "Brandy, yes, thanks, that would be nice," Dennis said, very aware of Angelina moving silently around the room.

She was at the window seat, fingering the pillows, then she turned. "Have we met before?" she asked the elderly lady a bit abruptly.

The lady smiled at her, a warm, kind smile. "We would surely remember if we had."

"Yes, I guess so," Angelina agreed softly, and she looked very tired suddenly and very endearing. Very endearing and producing overwhelming feelings of protectiveness in him.

"You two get comfortable. There are robes in the bathroom. Tea will be here soon..." she looked at

Dennis and winked "...with brandy, of course. Pleasant dreams."

Dennis followed her to the door and as she slipped out, he closed the door, then turned. Angelina was gone, but the door to the bathroom was open and he heard her moving around inside. The next moment, she came back into the room and frowned. "Cupids, Cupids everywhere."

"The lady does have a penchant for that little sprite, doesn't she?"

"Nauseating, isn't it?" she muttered and he would have laughed, but she seemed so serious right then. She looked at him with that same frown. "Do you want to use the bath in there, or the one down the hall?"

"You use this one. I'll go down the hall."

She didn't argue. She just went back inside and closed the door after her. Dennis kicked off his wet shoes, then stripped off his socks. He tugged the T-shirt off over his head, then took the shoes, socks and shirt closer to the stove and laid them on a small straight-backed chair to dry.

He took out his wallet and opened it. It was soaked. So was the money in it. He took the paper money out and laid the bills on the nightstand by the bed, then tossed his ruined watch next to them. It had stopped at one o'clock. No doubt the time he took that wild water ride down the bluff with Angelina.

He heard water start to run in the bathroom, and he turned to look at the closed door. Angelina was in there, taking off her dress, getting ready to soak in a hot tub, and he had no trouble visualizing any

of that. None at all. And his body responded immediately to those imaginings.

With a muttered oath, he laid his watch by the
wallet, then turned from the sounds, and left. This
wasn't going to be the easiest night of his life, that
was for sure.

ANGELINA STAYED IN the tub until the water grew
tepid and she felt as if she'd fall asleep at any moment. She finally climbed out of the old-fashioned
claw-foot tub and reached for one of the white fluffy
towels on a brass ring by the brass bowl provided
for a sink.

She looked at the gilt mirror with its wreath of
cherubs, and looked at herself. Her damp hair curled
wildly around her pale face, and she had faint shadows at her eyes. But the mud and debris were gone.
The only sign of the fall was the faint scrape on her
cheek. She looked very human, she thought. And this
place was making her feel very odd. The lady with
the spectacles seemed so familiar to her, yet there
was no memory she could pull up to match her. That
made her uneasy. She remembered everyone she had
dealt with, no matter how long ago. But not this human.

What bothered her more was the knowledge that
Dennis would be waiting outside the bathroom door
in the bedroom. A bedroom with one bed and little
more. But there were pillows, lots of pillows, and
she could build a wall of sorts down the middle of
the bed.

She reached for a robe hanging from a brass knob
on the back of the door and wrapped herself in the

incredibly soft material. She knotted the tie at her waist, then braced herself and stepped out into the bedroom. Her wish that Dennis wouldn't be there wasn't answered. He was not only there, he was sitting in the middle of the bed, wearing a robe just like hers, cradling a snifter of brandy.

His hair was slicked back from his face, still damp from the shower, but he hadn't shaved and there was the beginning of a new beard darkening his jaw. It made her literally hurt to look at him. All she wanted to do was get through this night, to not have this need in her to touch his jaw, to feel the beard. Or to gently smooth his hair back from his face. If she could just get through the night, she'd be thankful.

She crossed to the closest window seat to get the pillows, but before she could reach for one, he said her name.

"Angelina?"

She stopped, but didn't turn.

She sensed him moving, heard the bed creak, and knew he was coming over to her. She closed her eyes so tightly that colors exploded behind her lids. Don't let this happen, she begged silently. Please, help me.

He was there, so close she heard the breath he took before he said, "Don't you have anything to say?"

Her hands were curled tightly, her nails digging into her palms. "No."

"That's it?" he whispered hoarsely, his breath ruffling her damp hair.

"That's all there is."

"No, it's not. I told you I loved you."

"There can't be any more."

"Just tell me why?"

She bit her lip so hard she was surprised that she didn't taste the metallic pungency of blood on her tongue. "It's not meant to be. It's not in the scheme of things."

"That's ridiculous. Who knows what's in the scheme of things? This is my life, and I finally figured out what I want in that life. I want you in it."

She could feel the shaking beginning in her, and she hugged her arms around herself to try to stop it. "I can't be in your life." She took a rasping breath. "Don't you understand that?"

"All I understand is one thing." His words were low and rough, barely audible to her, and she knew she couldn't stop them. There was nothing she could do to keep him from saying it again. "I love you."

She swallowed hard, but nothing eased the tightness in her throat. "No," she whispered.

"Oh, yes," he said, then he touched her and it was all over.

He eased her around until she was facing him, and waited until she finally opened her eyes. He was there, so close, so dear to her, and suddenly she knew that every human emotion she'd experienced until that moment wasn't important at all.

He held her by her shoulders, his fingers tight, hovering just this side of inflicting pain, and she could see the uncertainty in his eyes. And it hurt when he finally whispered, "Just tell me that you don't love me, and I'll leave. I swear, I'll walk out of here. I'll sleep in the bathtub down the hall, and I'll let you go. Just tell me you don't love me."

Chapter Fifteen

Angelina had the words inside her, and she tried to say them. She tried to say she didn't love him, that she never had, but nothing in her could get those words out. She couldn't lie. She couldn't say she didn't love this human. She did.

"Just tell me," he whispered roughly, his fingers tighter now, compelling her to say something.

She would have given her own life right then to be able to dematerialize and go to the quiet place. To be away from here, away from Dennis and away from the damage she was doing to the only human being she'd ever loved.

"Either let me go, or let me love you," he said, each word breaking her heart bit by painful bit.

She lifted her hands and unsteadily touched his face. Love hurt. Love was the hardest thing in the world to experience, and yet at that moment, it was the most glorious feeling to touch him and to be touched by him. She drank in the look of him, the way his eyes were narrowed as if he expected pain to be inflicted. She touched his lips with the tips of her fingers, feeling the heat and life there, then said the words that sealed her fate forever.

"Love me, Dennis, just love me."

He stood very still, then he slowly moved his hand to cup the nape of her neck and he gently drew her to him. She was lost in the circle of his arms, holding him, knowing how crazy she was, but she didn't care. The only thing she wanted was Dennis. She tipped her head back to look at him, and his lips found hers. The moment she felt his mouth cover hers, there was no turning back.

She didn't know what she expected human love to be like, but in her it was frantic and needful and wonderful. The kiss was deep and searching, penetrating with heat and a power to draw the breath out of her body. She wound her arms around his neck, holding on to him, afraid that if she let go, this would all be gone. It would be snatched away from her before it began, and that terrified her.

Dennis buried his face in her neck, his lips burning her skin, then his hands found the knot on her robe and the tie was undone. In one easy movement, he had her in his arms, carrying her to the bed, and he gently laid her on the satin and rose petals.

When Dennis moved back, she reached out. She didn't want this sudden loss of touch, this sense of separation. But it only lasted for a moment. He shrugged out of his robe, letting the white terry cloth fall to the floor. And she saw him. A man. The man she loved. She knew it wasn't right to call a human male beautiful, but she couldn't come up with any other word.

His tanned skin was taut with a sprinkling of

darker hair dusting his chest and down to his stomach. She saw the need in him for her. It was heady to know that she could draw that response from him, to have him want her that badly. She held out her arms. "Please," she whispered unsteadily, and Dennis came to her, onto the bed, lying on the satin with her.

He faced her on his side, lifting himself on one elbow to look down at her, then he touched the terry cloth that covered her. Slowly, he pushed back the soft material, until she was all but naked. Her breasts swelled just from the touch of his gaze, her nipples peaking, and a sensation at her core came from nowhere.

"You're so beautiful," he breathed hoarsely, and that coiling of some sort grew in her, a pleasurably needy thing that almost exploded in her when his hand touched her stomach.

She gasped, arching to his touch, and when his lips found her nipples, she cried out. The pleasure was indescribable, part pain, part ecstasy, and it touched every atom of her being. It radiated like fire through her, and as his hand swept over her body, exploring and touching and teasing, the fire shifted to something that was almost unbearable. He cupped her hip, drawing her closer to his desire, pressing himself against her stomach, and she wound her legs around his.

So new, so wonderful and so overpowering. No wonder humans did silly, stupid things to be with the person they loved. To be touched by him, to be kissed by him, to be loved by him. She knew there was nothing she wouldn't do to be with Dennis, just this once. Somewhere deep in her soul, she knew it would never happen again, but for now, this was enough. This was her time, her memories that were being made to take with her to the quiet place when they drew her back from here.

Dennis shifted, moving closer to her, and she looked at him. She loved him with all of her being. The feeling was encompassing, pure and whole. She tugged him closer, tasting the sleek heat of his chest against her lips, tasting the heat and vague saltiness. Her hand trailed over his shoulders, along his back to his hips, then around to the front.

When she found his strength, he shuddered and arched toward her touch. He groaned, then she saw his jaw clench and she drew back quickly.

"I hurt you," she said, horrified.

He laughed, a rough, unsteady sound. "No, you didn't hurt me," he whispered. His hand shifted lower on her, and he splayed his fingers on her stomach. "You'd never hurt me," he said as his hand went lower. Then cupped her and she gasped and closed her eyes, the feeling sending shards of pleasure through her.

"Did that hurt you?" he breathed in her ear.

"N-no," she moaned. "No."

He moved the heel of his hand on her, slowly making circles. "How about this?"

"Oh, no, no," she breathed, barely able to get the words out when the feelings at her core robbed her of the ability to take air into her lungs.

"And you didn't hurt me," he whispered and touched her hand, then drew it to him again.

She circled him, held him, then slowly slid her

hand along his strength. He gasped, his eyes closed, and she could literally see his heart beating in his chest. Pleasure. It gave him great pleasure, but when she moved again, he stopped her.

His hand found hers and held, his other hand finding her sensitive core again. He moved on her, his fingers slipping into her heat, and she felt everything shatter. The connection was unbelievable, making her hips lift toward his hand, her head arch back. "Oh, oh, oh," she whimpered.

His hand was gone, and she cried out, but the next thing she knew, he was over her, his knees between her legs, his arms bracing him above her. "I want to be inside you," he said. "Now."

She felt him touch her, felt his strength press against her moist heat, then slowly he entered her. His hand had pleasured her, but this went beyond that. There was a pain, somewhere on the fringes, but the pleasure overlapped it, almost hiding it. With her eyes closed, she felt it all, yearning toward him, wrapping her legs around his hips to hold him to her.

With exquisite slowness he entered her, and finally, when he filled her, he hesitated. Her eyes opened, and she saw him over her, looking at her with a mixture of wonder and shock. "You're a virgin, aren't you?"

She felt fire in her face, the pleasure dissolving with each word he uttered. It was so obvious. She could barely look at him. "You're...you're disappointed?"

"No, I just...I never suspected. I mean, you're so beautiful, I just thought..." He was very still over her, not moving, and she didn't know what to do.

So she told him a truth that came from her heart. "I never met a human being I ever wanted to make love with before. I'm sorry."

"Sorry?" he gasped. "My God, you're wonderful. But I don't want to hurt you."

"Hurt me?" Nothing could hurt as much as him stopping like this. "If you want to stop..."

"Stop? Oh, no, I don't want to do that. I want you. I mean, I really want you. But I won't hurt you."

He moved slightly, and the feelings she thought had gone exploded in her. They'd been there all along, just waiting for him to move. "You won't hurt me," she managed to say in a breathless voice, and she moved her hips herself, lifting them toward him, keeping him deep inside her. "Please, just love me," she implored.

"Oh, that's the easiest thing anyone has ever asked of me," he said, then met her movement with his own.

The slowness was gone, the need too great, and he thrust into her. With each entry, she felt feelings that she didn't know could get any stronger without destroying her, feelings that grew more and more intense. She matched him, stroke for stroke, her fingers digging into his shoulders, keeping him closer and closer, as she felt her control catapulting away from her.

She loved him, she loved him. The chant came from her soul, as she climbed higher and higher with him, until there was nowhere to go, but to a place where there was just the two of them. A place where she became one with him. One. No division, no separation. One. And she let herself go as that place exploded into exquisite bliss. She heard voices cry out, then she tumbled with Dennis back, back, back until she was in his arms in the bed.

He stayed inside her for a long time, then withdrew and they rolled onto their sides facing each other. She snuggled in his arms, burrowing into his damp heat, and her last thought before she drifted off to sleep was the memories would never be enough. They'd have to be, but they'd always be pale images of the reality of being loved by this man.

IT WAS THE DREAM AGAIN, the woman coming toward him, his need for her staggering, then Dennis realized that he wasn't dreaming. It was reality. Angelina was there, her body against his, her leg lying over his thigh, and her breath brushing the skin over his heart.

It had been her all along. Angelina. But he had that dream long before he'd seen her at La Domaine. At least a month before. The dreams were so clear now, Angelina, his need for her, him wanting her. Now she was here. She was in his arms, her skin against his, and he was the first man she'd ever known.

He understood her fear now, her need to keep him at arm's length. Yet when she'd come to him, she'd been passionate and as needy as he'd been. She shifted against him, her hand moving to his stomach and his body tensed. As needy as he was right then. He'd thought he'd been sated, that loving her would satisfy him, but right then he knew that loving her would never be enough. Having her would never satisfy him. He wanted her over and over again, for the rest of his life.

She moved again, her breasts pressing against him, and he shuddered faintly at the intensity of the response she could incite in him. He lay very still, trying to settle, but it wouldn't go away. He turned a bit, pressed his lips to her hair and whispered, "Love?"

She stirred with a soft, "Mmm."

He stroked her arm with the tips of his fingers, felt her tremble, and knew she was awake. Her breathing caught slightly, the pattern disrupted, then she shifted back a bit, and in the shadows of the room, she looked up at him. "Sleeping?" he whispered.

"Not anymore." Her voice was soft and throaty, stirring him almost as much as her hand moving on his skin stirred him. She stroked his stomach, light feathery caresses and he drew a sharp breath. She pressed a kiss to his chest, then whispered, "I'm glad you woke me. I don't want to waste time sleeping."

"My thought exactly," he said with a smile.

"I need to tell you something, to let you—"

He pressed a finger lightly to her lips. "No talking. No explaining. I understand." He raised himself on his elbow and gently stroked her cheek, smoothing errant curls against her delicate skin. "I meant what I said. It meant a lot to me for me to be the one."

"I thought I knew a lot about love, but I'm so ignorant."

"No, you're wonderful." He leaned down and kissed her quickly. "You know, I had these dreams for about a month. Dreams about someone, a woman, a woman who was so desirable, so erotic, that I could hardly stand it. She drove me crazy and I never knew who she was...until now. She was you, all the time. You. And the reality is better than the dream, far better.''

''No, not me,'' she said, drawing back enough for him to feel a strange sense of abandonment that made no sense. She was still in bed with him, still lying with him, and all he had to do was reach out to have her.

''She was you, long before I met you. It doesn't make sense, does it? Unless it was a premonition, a foreshadowing of this moment. I mean, I even thought I saw her once when I was awake, like an apparition, in this long white gown...and curls.'' He touched her silky hair. ''Just like yours.''

She moved away from him onto her back and stared at the ceiling. ''No, you're imagining it. Humans imagine what they want life to be. They imagine the perfect moment, the time they'd like to put in a bottle and keep forever. But that isn't reality.''

He didn't want to hear this, not now. He went to her, shifting until he was over her, her body under his and the response of the contact was immediate. ''No, this is reality,'' he breathed, and tasted her lips. ''And this,'' he murmured as he trailed his lips along her chin to her throat. He gently eased her legs open, then touched her with his strength and she gasped softly. ''And this.''

He felt her heat and warmth, then her arms were around him, her legs lifting to circle his hips and she moved up to meet him. *Reality* was such a puny word to describe that moment. It was shattering, the culmination of a life alone, that moment when he was one with Angelina. Two are one. One. He filled her, felt her surround him, and before he could absorb the sensations, she moved her hips.

Any thoughts of soft and gentle were gone. Any thoughts of taking all the time in the world to experience her were gone. The passion exploded and demanded satisfaction, and she was as urgent in her motions as he was. He felt her fingers dig into his shoulders. He heard her gasp, arching back, and when the shuddering climax came, two voices cried out as one.

The world broke into such sheer joy that it was impossible to absorb it all. The only clear emotion in the shimmering cacophony he was experiencing was love. He loved her, and he drifted back, letting the feelings shimmer and disperse.

When she held on to him, snuggling into his side, and when he heard her softly sigh, he sank back into the bed. And as he drifted off into the world of sleep, he knew that he'd never have that dream again. Not when he had the reality right here.

Valentine's Day, 6:00 a.m.

ANGELINA WOKE with a start to the soft light of early dawn. For one brief moment, she thought everything was all right. She felt good, her sleep deep and wonderful, with a fantasy about... Dennis! Oh, no, that wasn't a dream. She could feel him against her, his heat along her side, and as she eased her eyes open, she knew what had happened.

Slowly, she opened her eyes all the way, darting a look around the huge room. All the cupids smiled down at her, but this wasn't a laughing matter. She'd done the most awful thing she could imagine doing. And she'd done it to the one human being she cared about.

Dennis moved against her, and she froze when desire rose in her. No, she couldn't want this man again. She should have never wanted him in the first place. She should have been strong.

But she'd been weak and stupid and it hurt. Her hurt was unimportant. What mattered was doing something to make things right for Dennis. Staying here wasn't an option. It had never been an option. It never should have been a reality. She turned just enough to see Dennis in the grayness.

Love. Oh, she loved him. She always would. No matter what happened, she'd make sure he was happy, very happy in this life. No matter what it cost her. She forced herself to move carefully away from him. To ease away from his hand on her, to untangle her legs from his, then she was free. And alone.

She carefully got out of bed and stood naked on the cold wooden floor then went into the bathroom. She picked up her ruined dress, shook it out and put it on. The soft sensuality of the material was gone, replaced by an uncomfortable scratchiness.

She turned and caught her refection in the mirror over the brass sink, pale and tense, her hair a halo of untamed curls. The dress held the smears of mud from last night and a small rip where the strap had broken. She was so different than she'd been when she first put this dress on. She turned away from what she'd become and eased the bathroom door open again.

She looked into the bedroom, saw Dennis still sleeping and tiptoed into the room. She crossed the room with agonizing slowness, terrified that Dennis would wake and she'd have to face him. But as she neared the bed, he sighed and it startled her. She froze, then slowly turned and saw he'd rolled over onto his back, the sheets tangled around his middle. But his eyes stayed closed, and with another sigh, he settled back into sleep.

She knew she should get out as soon as she could, but something drew her closer, and that same compulsion made her stand by the bed to just stare at him as the image of him sleeping filtered into her soul. Finally, she forced herself to turn away. She had to leave. She turned to the door, walked away and didn't look back.

She walked quietly along the hallway and down the stairs into the entry foyer. Not a soul was around. She crossed to the parlor, glanced into the old-fashioned room done in chintz, cabbage roses and antiques and spotted a phone on a spindly cherry wood table near the archway. She crossed and lifted the receiver, thankful when she heard a dial tone.

Information connected her with a taxi company, then a dispatcher was on the line, a painfully cheery person wishing her a good morning and anxious to serve her. But when she was asked for the address for pickup, she didn't know what to say. Then she saw business cards in a pink Cupid holder on a shelf just above the phone, right next to a delicate crystal Cupid.

Next to a red silhouette of Cupid, a flourish of script read ''The Victorian Inn, a place for lovers.''

She read the address right below it. "It's 2 Arrow Way," she said.

The dispatcher was silent, then asked, "Is that the right address? My chart doesn't show any homes or businesses up there."

She glanced around the old house that looked as if it had been there for ages. "I'm in the house right now. Just give your driver the address and tell him I'll meet him on the street. He's not to come up to the house."

"Certainly. He should be there in fifteen minutes."

Angelina put the receiver back on the cradle, then went into the foyer and crossed to the door. She'd just stepped out onto the porch when she sensed someone behind her. There were no sounds, nothing, but she could literally feel another presence. Her heart sank. There would be no zapping back to headquarters. But would they choose to confront her here, in the real world?

Slowly she turned in the open doorway and looked behind her, almost weak with relief when she didn't see Dennis or anyone from the Council. The elderly lady from last night stood by the bottom of the staircase, her hands clasped in front of her, her pale blue eyes behind the rimless glasses unblinking.

"We are up early," she said, but with none of the gentle smiles of the previous evening.

"Oh, I'm glad you're here. I really wanted to thank you for all your help last night."

Her pale eyes flicked over Angelina. "Oh, my, you did have a close call. That scratch. Very dangerous. Nature, that is. It can be very dangerous."

Nature was the least of her worries. Angela nervously tried to smooth the ruined fabric of her dress. "I have to leave."

"You cannot go anywhere looking like that. We surely can find you something else to wear."

"Oh, no, thanks." She felt the coldness of the new day at her back. "I called a taxi and they'll be here any minute. I can go home and change."

"Is there something wrong, my dear?" She came closer. "Do you want to talk about it?"

Talking would do no good at all. Getting out of here was the only thing to do right now. "I'm not trying to be rude, but I really have to get going. Thank you for everything you've done for us."

"And what about Mr. Benning? Is he leaving with you?"

"No, he's not. He's still sleeping."

She frowned slightly. "Are you sure you do not want to talk?"

"Positive. There's nothing to talk about. Life is life. It can't be changed. Even I know that."

"May we give you one piece of advice?" She didn't wait for Angelina to accept or decline. "Human beings are defined by those they choose to love."

"Choose. You don't choose who you love."

"Oh, but you do, even if that choice is made with your heart."

"I don't see how—"

"Oh, but you shall," she said, and patted Angelina on the arm, an oddly comforting contact. "You shall, my dear."

Then she reached in the pocket of her dress and

took out a tiny crystal Cupid. "Each guest gets one for a keepsake."

Angelina just looked at it, and shook her head. "Thanks, no," she said, but that feeling of knowing this woman was so strong right then, it was startling. But there was no memory attached to it. It only added to Angelina's sense of frustration, that and the little Cupid the woman kept holding out to her.

She murmured, "Goodbye," then stepped out into the clear morning light.

She turned back to the lady, but the door was swinging shut, and it closed with a muffled thud. She crossed the porch and went down the steps to the brick driveway where, off in the distance, past the meadow of grass, she could see the road. She headed toward it, and when she got there, she turned to look back at the house. It shimmered in the early morning sun, tall and imposing against the true blue of the sky. A place of magic. A place where she'd had one moment of real humanity.

She turned away from it and stepped out onto the shoulder of the road. The magic was over. It was all over.

Chapter Sixteen

Angelina looked into the distance down the road, and it was shimmering now, too. It took her a minute to realize nothing was actually shimmering. It was her eyes. She was crying. She swiped at her eyes, but that didn't stop the tears. They ran down her cheek, and made her throat ache, and by the time the taxi pulled up she had a pain in her head from crying.

The driver stopped, pushed the door open from the inside, and said, "You called a cab, lady?"

She nodded and scrambled inside. "Yes, I did—10 Mockingbird Ridge, please. There's a black car on the way down this road, parked to one side. I have to stop there."

"Sure thing, lady," he muttered and as she shut the door, he gunned the engine and took off with a glimpse in the rearview mirror. "You okay?"

She knew she looked horrible, in a ruined dress, bare feet and with her eyes probably all red and swollen the way humans got when they'd been crying. Right then, she wished she had a pair of those sunglasses she hated. "I'm okay," she said, knowing how much a lie that was.

"Sure. Strange place to be at this time of day," he said as he started down the hill. "Out in the middle of nowhere."

"I was at the inn for the night," she said, not about to explain about the accident to this man.

"What inn?"

"The one back there, in the old Victorian house."

"There ain't no—" He cut off his own words when they rounded a corner and the Bronco came into sight on the side of the road. "That your car?"

"That's it."

He pulled off the road behind the Bronco and she hurried out and over to the vehicle. The doors were unlocked and everything from last night was still there. She grabbed her purse, and oddly felt even more sadness at leaving the car. A piece of metal and rubber and glass. Yet she hated to turn from it and return to the cab.

Another layer of human grief, she supposed, as she hurried back to the taxi and got in.

"Got everything?" the guy asked.

"Everything I can take with me," she said as she sank back in the seat and he drove her away from everything she had shared with Dennis. From everything that made her human. Now she was going back to the cottage to wait for the Council and Miss Victoria to come for her and take her out of this existence. And maybe when she wasn't human any longer, the pain would stop.

DENNIS WOKE abruptly to silence and a heavy emptiness that he understood immediately. Angelina wasn't with him anymore. He had no sense of her around him, and when he sat up, the room was empty. He threw back the sheet and got out of bed. Quickly, he dressed in his clothes, damp shoes and pushed the now dry money back in his wallet, and shoved it along with his watch into his pocket. Then he hurried downstairs. But before he saw the elderly lady from the night before at the bottom of the stairs, he knew Angelina was gone.

"Where is she?" he asked. "Angelina. The lady I was with last night."

She looked a bit distressed, but her voice was calm, almost soothing. "She left...for now."

"She said she'd be back?"

"No, she will not be back here."

"But, you said—"

"She left. She said that she called a taxi service and she was leaving."

He sank down on the second stair from the bottom. She'd gone. Last night hadn't made any difference to her after all. "How long ago?"

"About six o'clock."

He looked at his bare wrist, then said, "What time is it?"

A huge grandfather clock he didn't remember seeing the night before, stood by the front doors and chimed ten o'clock right when he asked. He stood. "I need to get to my car. I wonder if I can walk to it?"

"One would think so. It must be only a short walk back down the main road. Easily within walking distance."

"Good," he said, then reached for his wallet. He took out two one-hundred dollar bills and handed them to her. "Is that enough for the room and everything?"

She looked at the bills and smiled. "Oh, Benjamin Franklin. A brilliant human being, but terribly eccentric." She glanced up at Dennis. "More than enough, thank you."

He turned to leave, but she spoke again and stopped him. "Mr. Benning, people only see what they are prepared to see. Ralph Waldo Emerson said that a long time ago. A very insightful human being."

He was certain this tiny woman was more than a bit off center. "Sure," he said.

"One more thing."

"What's that?" he asked, anxious to get going.

She put her hand in the pocket of her dress and drew something out, then held it toward him. A tiny crystal Cupid sat on her palm. "For you, sir, a small memento of your stay at the inn."

He almost smiled at that. A fat little guy in diapers. He took it, the crystal cool in his hand. "Thank you," he said, put it in his pocket, then turned and left.

The short walk the Inn proprietor had predicted turned into an hour hike. It was almost eleven o'clock when he reached the Bronco. He got in, saw that Angelina's purse was gone, but everything else was there. He reached for the cell phone, and saw a readout on the LED panel that he had messages. For one wild moment, he thought Angelina had left them, but that was soon crushed when he dialed in for them.

The first two calls were from Sam and Audry. Sam

wanted to make sure he was coming to his and Melanie's house that night for a Valentine's Day dinner, and Audry wanted to tell him that some man named Summers had been calling since the office opened to see if they had received a shirt. "What in the hell is he talking about?" she asked, then hung up.

The last message wasn't from Angelina, either. Lou spoke in his rough voice on the recording. "Kiddo, got that info for you. Re one Angelina Joy Moore. Sorry, but she doesn't exist. No nothing on the lady. Not even a Social Security number. The one she gave her boss belongs to a widow in Nebraska. I'll keep digging, but so far it looks as if she materialized out of thin air. Later."

Dennis hung up, then punched in Angelina's phone number. It rang ten times before he finally hung up and started the car. As he drove back down the hill, the phone rang again. He grabbed it on the second ring. "Yes?"

"Boss? Thank goodness. I was getting worried. No one's heard from you since your father saw you yesterday."

That seemed like a lifetime ago now. "Audry, I've been busy."

"I should have known. Work. You know, you need to get a life. Francine Clark just called to cancel lunch." He'd forgotten all about his appointment to have lunch with Francine. "And what's this about a shirt? That man just keeps calling about it."

"Ignore him." He looked at the clock in the dash. "Do me a favor. Call the florist and have roses sent to 10 Mockingbird Ridge."

"And what about the card?"

"No card. Just have them sent out right away. And have them send a dozen every hour until I tell you to stop them."

"It's your money," she muttered.

"Make sure they put a Cupid on them somewhere, okay?"

"You're the boss."

"I won't be in today. But if a Miss Moore calls, patch it through to this phone or my home phone."

"Oh, I see."

"See what?"

"Why Miss Clark canceled on you. Who would have ever thought?"

"Not even me," Dennis said.

A siren blared just as he turned onto the Coast Highway, and he glanced in the rearview mirror. Red-and-blue flashing lights.

"What's going on?" Audry asked.

"I'm getting a ticket," he muttered.

"What? What did you do?"

He didn't have a clue. He'd been concentrating on Angelina and getting to her, not his driving. "I don't know," he said as he eased off the road and parked on the dirt shoulder. He could see a cop getting out of the cruiser behind him. "I'll talk to you later," he said, hung up, then took his ruined wallet out of his pocket and rolled down his window.

The policewoman looked into the Bronco. "Benning, Dennis Benning?"

"Yes."

"You arranged to have a Volkswagen towed early this morning?"

"Yes."

"Could you step out of the car, sir?" She opened the door for him. "Just get out, and keep your hands where I can see them." Her other hand was resting on her holstered gun. "Now."

"What's going on?" he asked as he complied.

"Sir, you're under arrest for suspicion of grand theft auto."

"What?"

She removed her handcuffs from her belt and looked up at him. "We can do this the easy way, or we can do it the hard way."

Dennis couldn't believe any of this. Nothing in his life was making sense today, nothing. "This can't be happening. The car was a friend's car and—"

"The car was reported stolen in Nebraska a week ago."

6:00 p.m.

SHE WAS DREAMING for the second time in her human life. Yet she knew exactly where she was, in the cottage waiting for the judgment of the Council. And she loved Dennis.

She sank into the dream, an odd assortment of images of her time on earth, and all the dream was filled with Dennis. Dennis laughing, touching her, kissing her, just being there. And that time at the inn. She stirred, but the dream kept going.

"*Angelina,*" Miss Victoria whispered from the fringes of the dream. "*It is over. It is done. We are very pleased with you, with your heart and your soul. We shall miss you.*"

In the dream she was going somewhere, but she

didn't know where. It didn't make sense. "Where am I going?" she asked.

"You have finally found that place where you belong. Where you will be loved and shall love. That is all we ever wanted for you. Home, my dear, to the home you always were looking for."

"Home? Ma'am, I don't understand. I made such a mess of things. I hurt everyone. And Dennis, Ma'am, please take care of Dennis. Please."

"Dennis shall be just fine."

She shifted in the dream, a sense of foreboding starting to lift from her. If Dennis was happy, that's all she wanted. All she ever wanted. "Thank you." She knew that Miss Victoria never lied. "Thank you, Ma'am."

No matter what happened to her, *this* was settled. She sighed and let go of the pain in her. It would pass. It would eventually lessen and be bearable. *"We have to leave,"* the tiny woman whispered by her ear. *"It is over. Our time is done."*

"You have been like a daughter, a difficult daughter at times, but a cherished daughter. Now, go. Your destiny is waiting." The voice grew fainter and fainter, fading off into the grayness of the dream.

"She will not remember, will she?" the voice asked at a great distance.

Another voice came on the breeze. *"The child is not ours. Not anymore. She will not remember. She is a human now."*

Was that a sob she heard? No, the grayness was complete and a peace settled on Angelina. She was tired, so tired, maybe from all that work. Whatever it was, she snuggled into the softness of the bed and let sleep claim her.

THE TAXI DENNIS had hired passed Mockingbird Ridge twice before the driver finally spotted the sign and turned on the street. "Right there, over there," Dennis said, his total frustration surfacing against the poor driver. The man was chatty, but not very bright when it came to directions. What should have taken fifteen minutes from the police station had taken over half an hour.

But he finally saw the motor court in the gathering shadows of the coming night. When the driver pulled onto the driveway Dennis pointed to Unit A. "Here. Just park." He all but threw the money at him, hurried out and started for the door.

His footsteps faltered when he saw roses everywhere in front of the place, sitting on the porch, along the steps and by the door. All the roses he'd sent. And the house was totally dark. He stopped at the foot of the stairs, the sweetness of the roses in the air almost sickening to him.

She was gone. While he'd been rotting in jail, trying to prove he wasn't a car thief and trying to contact someone who could vouch for him, she'd left. "Dammit," he muttered, then heard a door open and close.

He glanced to his left and saw Mason coming out of the next unit. The man looked painfully fresh and cheerful, in contrast to his own rumpled appearance and frustration. "Hey, Mason?" he called out as he strode across the gravel. "Have you seen Angelina today?"

Paul turned and his smile was a bit forced. "Listen, there's nothing between us. I swear."

"I know. I know. I just need to reach her."

Paul glanced past him, then grimaced slightly. "Your flowers?"

"Yes."

"More trouble?"

"Yes. I just need to find her."

"I've been over there a couple of times today, but she's not there. And the florist has been knocking every time he brings a load, but I never saw her open the door. She must be out shopping or maybe she's at work."

She wasn't at La Domaine. He'd called there and been put in touch with an annoyed Summers. Angelina wasn't there, hadn't called in sick and was over two hours late for her shift. The man had been livid about it. "She's not at work. Do you know any of her friends or someone she'd be with?"

"No, I don't know much about her. Sorry." He flashed a look at his watch. "Hey, gotta go. If I see her, I'll steer her your way. Good luck."

Dennis muttered, "Thanks," as Paul turned and got in his truck. As he drove off, Dennis went back to Angelina's, stared at the dark cottage, then heard something. A muffled sound coming from somewhere behind the cottage. He moved toward the noise.

The low wall for the patio ran along the back of the cottage and as he approached an opening in it, a huge gray cat leapt out of the patio area and ran off into the night. Then he saw the French door, slightly ajar. He stepped over the wall, went toward the door and touched the frame. The barrier swung back quietly, and he could see inside.

She was there, on the bed, curled up sleeping. He was going mad and she was sleeping as peacefully as a kitten. He stood in the doorway just watching her, fighting a raw fear deep in his soul. He'd found her, now he had to figure out some way to keep her. He didn't know what to do.

His breathing caught when she stirred, then in the faintness of the moonlight that filtered into the room, he saw her move. She rolled onto her back, stretching her arms up toward the ceiling, and he gripped the doorjamb. "Angelina?" he whispered.

She froze, then suddenly was sitting up, her eyes wide as she saw him. "You...how...?" She rubbed at her eyes. "The dream. I thought..." Her hands stilled and she took a shuddering breath. "I'm so confused."

He would have laughed if there had been any room for humor in him. Right now, there was just the horrible certainty that the next few minutes were going to seal his fate.

"Why did you run away like that?" he asked, staying by the doorway, not trusting himself to get any closer.

She looked at him through the moonlight in the room. "I don't know," she said on a soft sob. "I don't know anything." She held out her hands to him. "Help me?"

He moved then, crossing to the bed and crouching down in front of her and took her hands in his. They felt cold and he laced his fingers in hers, holding tightly to her. "You help me."

"How?" she whispered and he could see her bottom lip trembling.

"Just love me."

He could feel her take a shuddering breath, then the next thing he knew, she was in his arms, holding on to him for dear life. She buried her face in his neck and he could feel her sobbing, hard, deep cries that shook his soul.

He eased back onto the bed, falling into the linens with her, but never letting her go. He closed his eyes tightly, sinking his hand into her hair and he whispered, "Love, don't cry. Please. Don't cry."

"You were gone and I was so alone." Her voice was muffled against his neck. "Don't leave me. Never leave me."

"You left me," he said, his own voice tight with emotion. "I woke up and you were gone. My God, do you know what that did to me?"

She took a sobbing breath. "No, I'd never leave you. I'd never, ever leave you. I couldn't. I couldn't."

He eased back, and looked down at her, her face damp from tears and her eyes wide with pain. Pain that he wanted to banish forever. "Why?" he asked, needing to hear her say those words.

Her hand lifted to touch his face, and she trembled convulsively. "Because I love you," she said, then miraculously she was smiling up at him. "Yes," she said more loudly. "I love you."

All the pain and raw hurt was gone and all that was left was Angelina and the life he always dreamed he'd have. He kissed her, needing the taste of her in him, then she came to him, completely and totally and the walls were gone.

There was nothing between them now, but love.

Later

ANGELINA LAY IN Dennis's arms in the tiny bedroom and just existed. That was it. She let life surround her and that life was Dennis. She didn't have to work at it. She didn't have to worry. She was there. He was there, and that was all that counted.

She settled in his arms, pressing her hand to his heart. She had so many questions, but answers weren't important just yet. Except one. "What took you so long to come?" she asked.

His hand stroked her shoulder. "I was in jail."

She was startled and lifted herself on one elbow to look down at him in the shadows of the bed. "What?"

"It's a long story, but I've been there since I left the inn. That Volkswagen your friend loaned you turned up stolen, and since I called for the towing, they thought I had something to do with the theft."

"Oh, my goodness, no. A Benning in jail? I bet your folks had a heart attack when they had to bail you out."

For some reason that made him smile. "I couldn't get in touch with them. Seems they went off on a cruise early this morning. The maid said they were acting strangely and said something about lost time."

"Who bailed you out?"

"I called the office, but the ever dependable Audry wasn't at work today. She left a voice mail that she and her husband were taking off for a long weekend in Carmel. I couldn't reach Sam or any of the Clarks, except Mrs. Clark. She was going to come down and bail me out, then the charges were suddenly dropped.''

"You're kidding," she said, tracing his nipple with the tip of her finger.

He drew a sharp breath and covered her hand with his, pinning it to his heart. "Stop that, or I'll never finish this story."

"Sorry," she whispered and touched her lips to the salty dampness of his shoulder. "Now, continue with the story."

"That's it. The car wasn't stolen, somebody got the numbers reversed, and that was that. It was like some conspiracy to keep me away from here until right now, this moment." His voice began to roughen when she kissed him again, and drew her hand back from his to trail it down to his stomach. "That does it," he breathed abruptly.

"What does what?"

"We have to get married."

Her hand stilled. "What?"

"Married. Any woman who can compromise me like this with just a touch, isn't a woman safe to be out in the world on her own." He chuckled roughly. "And you're definitely one human being who knows how to compromise me." He shifted toward her, inches from her face and touched her cheek. "Marry me, Angelina Moore? Be with me for the rest of our lives?"

She touched her lips to his, then drew back. "If you'll have me. Yes. I'll marry you."

"Have you? I love you, why wouldn't I have you?"

That confusion was there again, clouding the memories of her past. "I don't have any family," she said, and knew that for sure, but there were other things, blanks and fuzzy remembrances. "I'm not even sure if I..."

He pressed a finger to her lips. "No, I want you, not your family or your past. Just you. Be very sure of that. Do you understand?"

Something settled in her, a peace touched by incredible joy. "Of course. I'm a reasonably intelligent human being."

"Then understand this. You and me, forever. Agreed?"

"How romantic," she murmured, and drew him down into the bed with her again. "And how wonderful."

Epilogue

Miss Victoria turned away from the bedroom and drifted off to the quiet place. It really and truly was over. Angelina was not hers any longer. She was a human being, who loved and was loved.

"Why were you checking on Angelina?" a voice asked her from above.

She wasn't entirely certain why herself. "Humans tend to make such mistakes. We wanted to be certain that there were no mistakes with Angelina."

"Angelina is human now. She will make mistakes, but she will not be alone."

Miss Victoria took one last look at the tiny cottage and nodded with a smile.

"Victoria, the Mason-Clark intersection is doing well, but we are not so certain about the Bennings. Putting them on a cruise ship for two weeks seems to be a bit risky."

"Yes, one realizes how problematic that joining has been." Her only mistake had been hard to deal with for the past thirty-five years. Now, she had one chance to make it right. "But one feels if they are thrown together, if there is love, it will find a way."

"A cruise ship, with hundreds of humans on it, is hardly being thrown together. We must question the wisdom of that scenario."

"True, a cruise ship is crowded, but a deserted island where survival is imperative, why that would bring two difficult people together in a whole new way."

There was a stirring wind, then, *"Victoria!"*

"We cannot leave this up to Cupid," she said with a smile, then tossed something into the air.

It disappeared from her sight, then she heard voices. Angelina laughing, saying, "What is this?"

Dennis. "It looks like that Cupid the innkeeper gave me, but I thought it was in the car."

Angelina. "Cupid?"

Dennis. "I know, a fat little guy in diapers who shoots arrows. Sorry. She insisted I take it."

Angelina. "Don't be sorry. He's kind of cute. I think we'll keep him."

Dennis. "You never cease to amaze me."

"Amen," Miss Victoria whispered. *"Amen."*

Take 4 bestselling love stories FREE

Plus get a FREE surprise gift!

Special Limited-time Offer

Mail to Harlequin Reader Service®

> 3010 Walden Avenue
> P.O. Box 1867
> Buffalo, N.Y. 14240-1867

YES! Please send me 4 free Harlequin American Romance® novels and my free surprise gift. Then send me 4 brand-new novels every month, which I will receive months before they appear in bookstores. Bill me at the low price of $3.34 each plus 25¢ delivery and applicable sales tax, if any.* That's the complete price and a savings of over 10% off the cover prices—quite a bargain! I understand that accepting the books and gift places me under no obligation ever to buy any books. I can always return a shipment and cancel at any time. Even if I never buy another book from Harlequin, the 4 free books and the surprise gift are mine to keep forever.

154 HEN CE7C

Name	(PLEASE PRINT)
Address	Apt. No.
City	State	Zip

This offer is limited to one order per household and not valid to present Harlequin American Romance® subscribers. *Terms and prices are subject to change without notice. Sales tax applicable in N.Y.

UAM-696 ©1990 Harlequin Enterprises Limited

KEY TO MY HEART

Unlock the secrets of romance just in time for the most romantic day of the year—Valentine's Day!

Key to My Heart
features three of your favorite authors,

Kasey Michaels, Rebecca York and Muriel Jensen,

to bring you wonderful tales of romance and Valentine's Day dreams come true.

As an added bonus you can receive Harlequin's special Valentine's Day necklace. FREE with the purchase of every *Key to My Heart* collection.

Available in January,
wherever Harlequin books are sold.

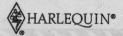

Don't miss these Harlequin favorites by some of our top-selling authors!

HT#25733	THE GETAWAY BRIDE	$3.50 U.S. ☐	
	by Gina Wilkins	$3.99 CAN. ☐	
HP#11849	A KISS TO REMEMBER	$3.50 U.S. ☐	
	by Miranda Lee	$3.99 CAN. ☐	
HR#03431	BRINGING UP BABIES	$3.25 U.S. ☐	
	by Emma Goldrick	$3.75 CAN. ☐	
HS#70723	SIDE EFFECTS	$3.99 U.S. ☐	
	by Bobby Hutchinson	$4.50 CAN. ☐	
HI#22377	CISCO'S WOMAN	$3.75 U.S. ☐	
	by Aimée Thurlo	$4.25 CAN. ☐	
HAR#16666	ELISE & THE HOTSHOT LAWYER	$3.75 U.S. ☐	
	by Emily Dalton	$4.25 CAN. ☐	
HH#28949	RAVEN'S VOW	$4.99 U.S. ☐	
	by Gayle Wilson	$5.99 CAN. ☐	

(limited quantities available on certain titles)

AMOUNT	$ _____
POSTAGE & HANDLING	$ _____
($1.00 for one book, 50¢ for each additional)	
APPLICABLE TAXES*	$ _____
TOTAL PAYABLE	$ _____

(check or money order—please do not send cash)

To order, complete this form and send it, along with a check or money order for the total above, payable to Harlequin Books, to: **In the U.S.:** 3010 Walden Avenue, P.O. Box 9047, Buffalo, NY 14269-9047; **In Canada:** P.O. Box 613, Fort Erie, Ontario, L2A 5X3.

Name: _____

Address: _____ City: _____

State/Prov.: _____ Zip/Postal Code: _____

Account Number (if applicable): _____

*New York residents remit applicable sales taxes.
Canadian residents remit applicable GST and provincial taxes.

Look us up on-line at: http://www.romance.net

075-CSAS

Look for these titles—
available at your favorite retail outlet!

January 1998
Renegade Son by Lisa Jackson
Danielle Summers had problems: a rebellious child
and unscrupulous enemies. In addition, her Montana
ranch was slowly being sabotaged. And then there was
Chase McEnroe—who admired her land and desired her
body. But Danielle feared he would invade more than just
her property—he'd trespass on her heart.

February 1998
The Heart's Yearning by Ginna Gray
Fourteen years ago Laura gave her baby up for adoption,
and not one day had passed that she didn't think about
him and agonize over her choice—so she finally followed
her heart to Texas to see her child. But the plan to watch
her son from afar doesn't quite happen that way, once the
boy's sexy—*single*—father takes a decided interest in *her*.

March 1998
First Things Last by Dixie Browning
One look into Chandler Harrington's dark eyes and
Belinda Massey could refuse the Virginia millionaire nothing.
So how could the no-nonsense nanny believe the rumors that
he had kidnapped his nephew—an adorable, healthy little boy
who crawled as easily into her heart as he did into her lap?

BORN IN THE USA: Love, marriage—
and the pursuit of family!

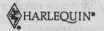 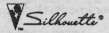